Without Head
or
Tail

A Novel

Maria Zuckerman

Author's note

Without Head or Tail is a novel that focuses on the Dominican-Haitian reality in order to provide viable solutions to a national problem with serious international repercussions. The novel has no political overtones.

It is a fictionalized account of Dominican-Haitian relations from 2010 to 2017. It has been written for the inhabitants of Hispaniola — in other words, for Haitians and Dominicans. The account has omitted the names of the government officials of the Dominican, Haitian and American administrations who were in office during that period of time, except for the names of Presidents Joaquin Balaguer and Jean-Bertrand Aristide in order to provide a point of reference to that period of time in Haitian-Dominican relations.

Without Head or Tail falls within the category of fiction, but only with respect to its characters whose interactions comprise the plot of the story based on information I obtained from reliable national and international sources, Dominican laws, rulings, treaties, conventions, books, local press articles, and essays. How Dominicans and Haitians feel about immigration matters is portrayed through the thoughts and concerns of the main characters.

Therefore, while the information in this novel is not of my authorship, the way it is presented is. It follows a simple, objective, linear account of events despite the lengthy gaps of time between the creation of immigration laws and their implementation and enforcement by Dominican authorities.

Because this work focuses on such issues as national sovereignty, what it means to be a Dominican, the solidarity between Dominican and Haitians, economic cooperation, and the reclaiming of values necessary for both societies, other important and complicated issues of Dominican-Haitian relations were not explored in depth, but were simply mentioned in passing, such as illegal trafficking along the Dominican-Haitian border. I deliberately skimmed over these issues so as not to divert my readers' attention by adding controversy on top of the controversial matter that is immigration. Sacrificing their discussion does not diminish the intellectual value of my work; much less does it imply that it was produced lightly or irresponsibly.

Without Head or Tail has been written in a dynamic, objective, respectful, and edifying manner with the intent of raising the consciousness of Haitians and Dominicans and an understanding that peace, harmony, economic development, and the resolution of Hispaniola's major issues rely on the collective goodwill of all, the cooperation of both governments, and on the responsible behavior of Dominicans and Haitians as people of integrity in their day-to-day living.

Lastly, I wish to point out that I included the image referenced by the characters of a mythological creature with regenerative and healing powers as a metaphor, to define the new relations that must occur between the two countries, since the old wounds shared by Haiti and the Dominican Republic must be cured before understanding and respect can flourish between them.

Maria Zuckerman

It sprang from the bowels of the island like a germinating seed gone mad. It burst forth with great force, opening up the soil like a giant mouth to swallow whatever was on the surface.

Nobody saw what escaped from the center of the earth; only the devastation it left behind.

Some eyewitness accounts described a two-headed dragon. Others said it was the Devil himself who'd escaped from Hell, careening in a cloud of smoke toward the Caribbean, taking the souls he wanted with him.

These things the survivors agreed upon: that it was all over, that they had to flee, and their only option, if they wished to live, was to walk toward the land of the rising sun.

The gray cloud of dust that arose over Port-au-Prince minutes after the catastrophic earthquake of Tuesday, January 12, 2010, announcing to the world the tragedy that had occurred, became heavier with each building that collapsed, giving the city a phantasmagoric look. The earthquake, which registered a 7.0 on the Richter scale lasted 35 seconds; enough time to destroy the Haitian capital, shake the Dominican Republic, Cuba, and Jamaica, and trigger a tsunami alert for the entire Caribbean region.

Survivors looked like beings who had escaped from the grave. They ran about in despair, covered in dust, screaming and invoking the protection of saints and spirits, seeking a safe haven that did not exist. The call to aid the wounded and those trapped under the rubble was intermingled with the shouting and commotion.

The earthquake's 44 aftershocks only served to heighten the prevailing confusion and chaos. The few buildings that had remained erect in the city continued to fall like dominoes, and streets and roads disappeared into crevasses opening up with a deafening sound, leaving the inhabitants of Port-au-Prince isolated and helpless. Was it the end of Haiti? Not only the Haitians, but the whole world wondered.

****

"Let's open the borders so the wounded can be brought to different hospitals to be treated here. Send trucks to Haiti with food, medicine, and first aid kits as well as medical equipment. Also, we've got to provide assistance to the Haitian population with restoring their telecommunications, power, and transportation system," the Dominican president instructed his cabinet, gathered in an emergency session after he had verified the devastation of Haiti in person.

"The whole world is in solidarity with Haiti. Reconstruction assistance has already been promised," said the Dominican public health minister.

"I know," the Dominican president responded, "but since we are the closest, our help will be the first to arrive in Haiti, and we will be the first to assist Haitians with whatever they need. Moreover, the airport of Port-au-Prince is destroyed, and the roads to the airport no longer exist, so all international aid will have to be channeled through us."

"This action will give your administration a very good image internationally; it will play up the humanitarian work of the Dominican Republic in this tragedy and our spirit of cooperation with other nations," uttered the secretary of state as if he were prophesying a promising future.

"All that is well and good, but let's not forget our own reality. Our law enforcement must be reinforced to keep these people from crossing the border into our country without documentation," the minister of police pointed out, addressing his colleagues with grave tone and pragmatism. "I have already sent orders to place more surveillance along the border from Monte Cristi to Pedernales to prevent a Haitian stampede into our territory."

"I understand your concerns. Those details should be coordinated simultaneously with the departments of defense and state, all right?" the Dominican president replied, standing up to indicate that the emergency cabinet meeting was over. "What matters now is that our assistance reaches Haiti immediately, and that we are also ready and able to provide it in our own territory."

****

"Blessed Virgin! Matilde, have our staff improvise any spot they can in this facility and nearby for treating the injured," ordered the director of the small hospital in Jimaní when he saw another caravan of buses approaching the facility with more injured Haitians. The public hospital building, located in the southern border province of Independencia, was a veritable hive of local and international rescue squads, doctors, and volunteers, where national and international assistance to Haiti was being coordinated.

"But, doctor, that's precisely what we've been trying to do since this sea of people started to arrive. Literally, we have to look where we're walking, otherwise we'll step on them. We're constantly setting up tents to treat patients according to their injuries, but we just can't keep up," answered Matilde Ramirez, the hospital's administrator and manager of operations, in a rush.

Pearls of sweat were sprinkled across Matilde's forehead. Strands of her thick chestnut-colored hair had begun to wander out of the bun at the nape of her neck. Physical exhaustion was evident in the dark circles under her sad, honey-colored eyes and the heaviness of her movements. A woman of dainty features, short height, and clear complexion, her plump figure moved with difficulty in the maelstrom of doctors and paramedics providing non-stop assistance to the victims.

"True," the hospital director answered. "Thank goodness the president ordered the public health minister to have the critical patients be transferred to other medical centers in the country, otherwise, this situation could be worse. We can't even handle this tragedy now, not even with the international aid stationed here and in Haiti."

"This place looks like a battlefield," Matilde muttered under her breath, struggling to find words to describe the horror they were facing each day. "Doctor, every day we've been performing up to 60 limb amputations due to gangrene and assisting up to 700 people with pelvic and cranial fractures – they're being referred to other hospitals but still, I don't know how we're treating that many."

"Send Pascual to the town hall as soon as possible to have them come and help us with this. Make sure the bodies and this mountain of amputated limbs are buried in a mass grave," the hospital director told Matilde. He was scanning the overflowing anthill of humanity for Pascual Jiménez, the young volunteer from the Santiago Fire Brigade. Pascual had become indispensable for his uncanny gift of appearing as if he were an angel when help was most needed. Matilde struggled to be heard in the cacophony of incessant complaints, calls for help from injured patients, and requests for medicines, antiseptics, antibiotics, bandages, and other medical supplies from the doctors and paramedics.

"We're sitting in a powder keg, Doctor," Matilde commented. The overcrowding and the precariousness of our position are working against us. Let's pray it doesn't rain, because if it does, we are in big trouble." The hospital director nodded to her in acknowledgment, silently thanking God that it was not the rainy season. They were all exhausted and could not take one more obstacle.

Given the magnitude of the earthquake in Port-au-Prince that left a total of 316,000 dead, over 350,000 injured, and around 1,500,000 affected in other ways, the humanitarian aid was like a single drop of water lost in the vast ocean of blue tarps that covered the Haitian capital. There were only misery and pain. The challenge was made all the more formidable by the fact that the Haitian government could no longer govern, having been deprived of all the buildings where it could have operated and met to impose organization on the chaos that now defined everyone's life in Haiti, and above all, properly channel the international aid the Haitians were receiving.

This overwhelming tragedy, need, and helplessness brought Haitian and Dominican authorities together to work hand-in-hand. The leaders of the two nations understood that it was the only way to overcome the terrible predicament that Haiti, and by extension, the entire island of Hispaniola was in. This did not go unnoticed in the United States.

During a July 12, 2010 press conference in the Oval Office of the United States White House, the American president had encouraging words for the Dominican president, his distinguished guest: "One of the first messages I wanted to deliver was my appreciation for the role that the Dominican Republic played in helping the international community respond to the crisis in Haiti after the devastating earthquake there. And I think that the Dominican Republic's role, [its president's] role in particular, in helping to facilitate a rapid response was extraordinarily important. It saved lives and it continues as we look at how we can reconstruct and rebuild in Haiti in a way that is good not only for the people of Haiti but also good for the region as a whole."

"We are satisfied with the cooperation and understanding we now have with our Haitian friends. The suspicions of the past have been left behind," said the Dominican president, filling with pride as he recalled what his foreign minister had said during the emergency cabinet meeting held in January immediately after the earthquake. A smile spread across his face. In truth, it was an historical moment and he was the main character. The island, a ship gone adrift, now seemed to be headed for a safe harbor under his collaborative direction to rescue Haiti, and the whole world was witnessing it.

However, the taste of victory was very short-lived. Three months after the Dominican president was recognized in Washington, D.C., on October 11th, 2010, the ship he captained began to take on water. The devil who never sleeps came from Asia in the form of an epidemic of acute diarrhea and vomiting along the Artibonite River one hundred kilometers west of Port-au-Prince, an area not seriously affected by the earthquake. The American Centers for Disease Control and Prevention and the Pan-American Health Organization confirmed cholera in Haiti. It had been over 50 years since the last outbreak.

"I don't give a damn what the spokesman of the World Health Organization says about the strain of the virus coming from Nepal or whether the UN Stabilization

Mission is responsible for this epidemic!" the Dominican president snapped at his health minister. "Coordinate joint actions with the Haitian health minister to prevent this cholera from spreading."

"Yes, I've already communicated with him and an educational campaign will be launched in 24 hours." The Dominican health minister proceeded to explain the campaign, which was to focus on prevention through education in the areas of water use, food handling, sewage, hygiene, and community sanitation.

Once the President heard the details, he rose from his chair and began pacing back and forth frenetically like a caged lion. The vulnerability of the Dominican nation loomed large. The Dominican Republic was walking on a tightrope with the cholera outbreak in Haiti.

"Summon the tourism minister immediately!" the president ordered his secretary. "We need to start an international campaign to protect our tourism industry. It's essential for the foreigners visiting our country to feel safe; they must understand that the cholera outbreak is at the other end of the island, not here."

The Dominican president stood still for a few seconds. Then he leapt into action, moving quickly to his desk, grabbing the telephone, and giving orders to various staff members in a sharp, aggressive tones. Thoughts instantly arose in his mind of possible scenarios that could arise in the imminent war against cholera, and he had to be prepared for combat.

"Here we are, like Aquemichú, the stubborn donkey who took one step forward and twenty-four backward," muttered the President, releasing his frustration by slamming the receiver down on the telephone.

****

2

At Dario Contreras Hospital in Santo Domingo, the medical staff were doing their best to treat and stabilize Haitians with pelvic and hip fractures and other serious types of orthopedic trauma.

Among them was a tall man who appeared to be about 45 years- old. He suffered from a multitude of fractures all over his body. After surgery, he was transferred to one of the recovery shelters that had been set up in Santo Domingo. The patient, despite the painkillers that had been administered to him, continued to complain and kept repeating incoherent phrases.

"This poor man," explained Nurse Gisela Morales to Nurse Saul Pimentel, who had come in to relieve her that morning, "was rescued from under the wall of a building that collapsed. No one understands how he's still alive. His constant babbling is causing a bit of confusion."

"How? What's he saying?"

"I have no idea! In his half-Creole, half-Spanish jibber-jabber, he keeps referring to a sugarcane mill. I'm sure he's delirious. He's suffering from a high fever due to a urinary tract infection. Let's hope there are no more complications, given all the traumas he's presenting. We have to keep him under close observation."

"Understood," said Nurse Pimentel, writing some notes on the papers attached to the foot of the patient's bed.

****

"Don't take me! I work here, I work here!" shouted Pierre Selvandieu as he ran in a panic among the reeds at the Consuelo sugarcane plantation, screaming as if he had seen the Devil. He was trying to escape from the Dominican National Police agents pursuing him in the raid they had undertaken to execute Executive Decree 233 of June 13, 1991, ordering the repatriation of all undocumented Haitians under the age of 16 years or over the age of 60.

Police officers were emerging all over the place like ants from a stepped-on anthill, communicating with each other via walkie-talkies to find and capture the undocumented Haitians in the area, who offered no resistance once apprehended.

Pierre knew the terrain like the back of his hand, so he tried to calm down. He glided through the reeds with the swiftness of a water moccasin. The police, however, still picked up his trail. The strong smell of Pierre's sweat, made even sharper by the rush of adrenaline that drove him onward, had betrayed him.

A band of agents stationed at the entrance to one of the main roads of the sugarcane plantation stopped Pierre. Exhausted from fleeing through the endless labyrinth of reeds, he gave himself up and joined the group of Haitians already captured by the police officers.

"Colonel, we've stopped about 20 children and 100 adults. The trucks carrying these people back to Haiti will be headed out this very night," reported Captain Zepeda.

"Excellent! I'll tell the Secretary of Police to inform his Excellency, Dr. Balaguer, that we've carried out the provisions of the order." The Colonel, puffed with smug satisfaction, imagined the recognition he would receive for his performance.

The delirious Haitian lying in the bed at the recovery shelter kept bringing the past into the present, shouting one reason after another to not take him away. Nurse Pimentel approached him with a syringe and injected him with a sedative.

****

3

The earthquake in Haiti forced the government authorities of the two nations to plan and act as they went along. To stay afloat, ad hoc measures were taken as problems arose. It was like placing little Band-Aids to hemorrhaging wounds that seemed to bleed the island to death on both sides. Some officials began to worry about the future repercussions of the reactive approach of the two island governments.

"Dominican schools are receiving Haitian students who were left without schools in Haiti. This was a predicament limited to the provinces along the border, at first. Now, however, Haitians are flooding our schools and universities here in Santo Domingo."

"We expected that to happen. What's your point?" the Dominican president said to his education minister, unable to understand what his minister was getting at.

"Of course! What really worries me is that these students have no documentation and this will further complicate the immigration situation, which is delicate enough as it is. I understand this measure is temporary, that we're allowing it for humanitarian reasons due to dire circumstances among our neighbors. But, we all know Haiti's reconstruction will take many years, and in the meantime, we Dominicans will be the ones carrying the burden ..."

"These issues are being coordinated with the Haitian authorities, who in turn are following the instructions of the Haitian President. The eyes of the world are fixed on what the Dominican and Haitian governments are doing during this crisis. The international community is giving us their support."

The Minister of Education understood by the president's terseness that he had more pressing matters to address, so he asked permission to leave, and departed in silence, even more worried than when he had stepped into the president's office to speak with him. The meeting was useless. Was he the only one clearly seeing what was going on?

He left the National Palace with a head full of statistics he could not afford to show to the President.

We have to do something to keep this situation from getting out of hand. We have 56,000 Haitian students in our public and private schools. 44,000 in our elementary and high schools, 12,000 in our universities. Of the 67% of our national student population who are foreign students, Haitians represent 66%. Um, these statistics are nothing to sniff at. Our identity as Dominicans is being diluted due to the overwhelming penetration that has been allowed for reasons of solidarity. And the nation's sovereignty is disappearing under the pressure of all these international organizations. Where in the hell are we headed?

It's good to support each other, but considering the circumstances, the Dominican Republic has to reinforce our national curriculum to emphasize our history, our cultural heritage, our national values, so our young people will know who they are and will be proud of it. Being a Dominican means more than obtaining Dominican nationality for being born here, and it means more than getting citizenship for living here. Please, let this solidarity not lead to our nullification ...

****

The heat was overpowering. The blue tents felt like ovens, trapping the hot air inside them. The Doctors, nurses, and volunteers did all they could to keep the patients hydrated and comfortable.

"Doña Matilde, please come with me." Pascual looked as if he had seen a ghost and his face was shadowed with great distress.

"You look white as chalk, what's wrong?"

"We have an outbreak of diarrhea and vomiting among our patients ..."

Matilde crossed herself at the news. She felt as if her soul had slipped out of her body for a moment. She fixed her gaze on the wall of the area where she was working, an improvised corner where Jimaní's medical services were being coordinated.

"Alert the epidemiological team, have them check for cholera." And without even looking at Pascual, she went out into the front area of the hospital in search of the director. He would be the one responsible for alerting the authorities to what was going on, and everything seemed to indicate that cholera had come to the Dominican Republic.

What Matilde didn't know was that the epidemic had already shown up in other parts of the Republic. The issue was at the top of the agenda for the president's meeting with the education minister in the morning. With cholera in the Dominican Republic, the ship that he captained could go down with this new development.

The bomb was dropped by the public health minister in the president's office just 45 days before Christmas, at the start of the high season for travel to the Dominican Republic. The minister tried to remain calm, but as he was a doctor by profession, no one knew the gravity of the matter better than he.

"It was a question of when it was going to happen, not whether it was going to happen, Your Excellency," explained the public health minister. "This strain of the virus is resistant to antibiotics. From what we've seen in Haiti, we cannot use trimethoprim-sulfamethoxazole, furazolidone, Neggram, or streptomycin to control the spread of it in our territory. None of these antibiotics work."

"What a fucking year!" exclaimed the Dominican president. "It started on the wrong foot and is going to end on the wrong foot. Properly notify the press to avoid panic. The population must not get agitated. Make it happen."

However, as soon as the president had issued his orders, the fires of hell immediately began to burn the public health minister and the Dominican government. The information was leaked before the public health minister had even left the National Palace.

"Mr. Minister, how will the government cope with this new crisis?" reporters from multiple television channels and the press asked in unison while videotaping and photographing the official's reaction as he walked into the public health ministry.

"Actions are being taken to mitigate and prevent the effects of cholera in the country. We will have the help of the agencies of the United Nations. We are also working with the minister of education and other public and private institutions to implement actions at the community and school levels in accordance with each area's needs and requirements."

"Doesn't it seem like a very vague plan for what we have to face? According to international sources, 500 people have died of cholera in Haiti to date and 7,359 have been hospitalized due to the virus," one of the newspaper reporters pointed out provocatively during the improvised press conference.

"I told you the plan of action we have for our affected and at-risk populations. Enough questions for now!" The public health minister swept into the building, leaving behind the hornet's nest of journalists who insisted on loaded questions to trip him up and trick him into revealing confidential information.

The news of cholera in the Dominican Republic hogged all the headlines of the nation's major newspapers. On the one hand, they sounded the alarm to the population about the severity of the virus, yet on the other hand, they published the opinions of health experts, who called for caution and staying calm, and of grandstanding Dominican politicians, who pointed fingers at the different parties they believed to be responsible for the outbreak of the virus on the island and demanded solutions.

In the beginning, 11 to 13 new cases of cholera were reported daily. By the second half of December, cholera cases had quadrupled. In Santo Domingo, it affected the neighborhoods adjoining the Ozama River. It also spread to Santiago and Cibao Central, the border regions and the southwest, to Elías Piña, San Juan, Dajabón, Azua, and Independencia.

Despite the panic and shock caused by the news of the cholera epidemic, the situation remained under control thanks to the National Epidemiological Surveillance System and the cooperation of the Dominican population. Fortunately, tourism hubs were not affected, and no recommendations were issued for restrictions on travel or trade with other countries or with the different regions was affected by cholera.

****

4

Three cargo trucks guarded by troops of the Dominican National Police took the journey toward Haiti transporting the Haitians who were detained in the raid. They were crowded into the railed beds of the trucks like cattle. The trucks stopped several times along the way to rest. As soon as the trucks reached the border, the Haitians were released. They stepped off the trucks as if they were passengers whose buses had let them off at their chosen stop.

"Come on, come on! Move!" ordered Captain Zepeda. The other policemen, wearing black helmets and carrying high-caliber weapons, flanked the Haitians as they crossed the border to ensure an orderly, quick passage.

The Haitian police, standing on the other side of Elías Piña, let their countrymen cross the border into Haiti without even bothering to check their names. But that night, instead of allowing them to go their own way, as was the custom, they were led to a special place where they were interrogated.

"Pierre Selvandieu, you said your name was?" asked a Haitian officer in Creole while another officer functioning as an assistant took down the information.

"Yes, sir."

"Aren't you too young to work in the sugar mills?" The officer was staring at Pierre. His limbs were muscular, but his smooth face and gawky teenager's bearing belied his youth.

"This guy named Simon stopped me one day in the street to ask me if I wanted to work in Dominican. He told me I'd be paid good money and, well, I said yes, and in a few days a guy picked me up one night near Tirolí and..."

"That's enough! Release this wretch!" the officer barked to his assistant.

No information on the illegal trafficking of Haitian minors by Haitians into the Dominican Republic could appear in any documents presented by Haitian authorities to international organizations as evidence of the abuse of Haitians in the Dominican Republic.

Decree 233 of June 13, 1991, ordering the first of a series of mass repatriations, was President Balaguer's first swift response to allegations of abuse and mistreatment of Haitians made by a non-governmental organization on June 11, 1991, with the consent of Haitian President Jean-Bertrand Aristide, before the United States House of Representatives. These mass repatriations in turn triggered a series of investigations by the Special Delegation of the Inter-American Commission on Human Rights of the Organization of American States to verify the alleged abuses.

While she was attending to the patient lying next to the Haitian with serious multiple injuries, Nurse Gisela Morales overheard the latter whisper the name "Pierre Selvandieu." She wrote it down in his record, followed by a question mark. The Haitian remained stable despite his delicate condition.

****

5

"The patient with multiple fractures is awake now. He hasn't presented any fever in the last 24 hours. He's anxious, but that's normal. He insists on talking to the doctor," Nurse Pimentel reported to Dr. Rojas as they made the rounds of the shelter. The doctor went to the room where they were keeping the patient, whom they described as "the Haitian who won't stop talking." Saul Pimentel followed the doctor into the room; he was the Haitian's attending nurse now that Nurse Gisela had finished her shift.

"You look better," commented the doctor as he took the medical records Nurse Pimentel handed to him. "Um... The only information we have for you is that you were rescued from under a wall five days after the earthquake. We don't have your name." The doctor looked over the patient's medical records, but before Dr. Rojas could open his mouth to inform him about his current condition, Pierre began sharing his odyssey.

"I am Pierre Selvandieu. I was selling my fruit in the Port-au-Prince Market when a huge noise and a jolt threw me and all the fruit to the ground. I thought the ground was opening up, but it was the buildings toppling over. I woke up, and then I fell asleep again; the earth swallowed me alive. I told myself, I'm not gonna die here, I'm getting out of here."

"Well, one could say you are alive thanks to your determination and your strong mental attitude, because you have multiple pelvic fractures, a broken leg, and multiple broken ribs. On top of that, you have had serious bladder trauma and respiratory infections, but you have overcome those as well. All in all, you're making a miraculous recovery. We just have to keep you stable to avoid further complications. Your recovery process is going to be a long one. I must inform you that your left leg will be permanently two inches shorter than the right, due to the pelvic trauma you've suffered. You'll also probably have permanent bladder issues."

Pierre looked down at his legs, absorbing what the doctor had said. He clenched his jaw and took a painfully dry swallow. For him, the worst was over.

****

Three months later, Pierre Selvandieu was authorized to be discharged. He had earned the admiration of the entire staff for his resilience. All of them considered it a miracle that Pierre had survived the earthquake and his terrible injuries.

"Mr. Selvandieu, keep in mind that being discharged doesn't mean you can abuse yourself. You have to relearn many things, starting with walking. It is important you continue to strengthen your leg muscles, gluteal muscles, and your core with the exercises we've taught you." Nurse Pimentel stopped, wondering to himself if the Haitian had understood what he said.

Pierre was playing with his hands as Nurse Pimentel gave him his final instructions. For a while, he gazed up at the sky blue walls and the white cornices crowning the ceiling of the room, paying little attention to what Nurse Pimentel was telling him. In his mind, he was saying goodbye to a refuge as peaceful and heavenly as the soft blue of its walls. He was going to miss this place, the care he had received, but most of all, he was going to miss the security and safety he had enjoyed for three months.

"Do you have any questions?" asked Nurse Pimentel.

"No," answered Pierre with a knot in his throat. He wasn't the type of man who could be easily daunted. But he had to accept that he wasn't the same man he was before. Returning to Haiti was unthinkable, as it was still in a hellish condition. He rose to his feet with the help of his crutches and slowly and awkwardly headed down the hallway towards the entrance of the shelter. He had already made up his mind to stay in the area, no matter what. Staying near a hospital was essential so that he could cope with the terrible pain his pelvic fractures had caused, as well as the limitations he now had with his bladder.

****

6

Gabriel Novoa Ramírez was a born leader who had studied law at the State University of Santo Domingo. He had also studied political science, international law, and constitutional law at the master's and post-graduate levels. To gild the lily, he was also adept at foreign languages and was fluent in Creole, English, and French.

He had inherited his mother's honey-colored eyes and thick chestnut hair. He had cinnamon-colored skin, a taller-than-average height, and a slender swimmer's build. He had a wide smile which lent a gentle kindness to his angular face. He also had a charismatic personality with a strong dash of restlessness.

In his professional practice he directly witnessed the problems the Dominican Republic was facing as a result of the international allegations of abuse of Haitians, and the investigations being conducted in the country after Haitian President Jean-Bertrand Aristide had protested the alleged abuse and requested aid from the United Nations to deal with the untimely mass repatriations of Haitians ordered by President Balaguer's government.

As a lawyer for the Dominican department of state, he was privy to the official letters sent by the Dominican government to the OAS and the UN during President Balaguer's administration, defending its position as a sovereign nation. He also saw the records of the mass repatriations of Haitians executed by current government. And above all, he was well aware of the international campaign some countries had launched to unify the Dominican Republic and Haiti because they believed that unification was the only way to prevent mass migrations.

"You seem preoccupied, Gabriel," commented Ambassador Martinez Durán. "Is there anything I should know, anything I can do to help you?"

"Your Excellency, I appreciate that. You're right, I am worried; but what worries me isn't related to my work. I'm feeling unsatisfied, a little restive under the circumstances ..." He spoke in confidence, not only to his personal friend and former professor, but to a respected legal expert and diplomat who not only advised the current foreign affairs minister, but had served as chief of legal affairs in the chancellery for many years. Ambassador Emilio Martinez Durán was himself an institution of the Dominican chancellery.

"Why don't you come home with me tonight at 8:00? I have no official duties tonight, so we can talk about your concerns over dinner. Sandra will be very happy to have you with us."

"I will be there, Your Excellency. Thank you."

The ambassador had been Gabriel's professor while he was studying for his master's degree in diplomacy and international law, and they had been close friends ever since. Sandra, the ambassador's wife, had grown fond of her husband's former student, now his protégé in the department of state.

Gabriel showed up at the agreed time carrying a bottle of wine and a box of chocolates, his hostess's favorites. A man of small stature, white hair, a small mouth, prominent nose, and furrowed face and neck that spoke eloquently of his lengthy legal and diplomatic career, Ambassador Martínez Durán opened the door. Almost instantly, Doña Sandra Ledesma de Martínez, a beautiful woman whose face and figure hinted nothing of the many years marriage she had shared with Don Emilio, appeared by her husband's side.

It was not until after dinner, when Doña Sandra had retired to her room, that Gabriel finally felt comfortable sharing his feelings with the ambassador in the living room.

"Don Emilio, don't take me wrong or think I'm ungrateful. But I've been feeling for months like … well, like I'm in the wrong place. At first, I thought I was just upset over how the immigration situation was handled internationally and I feel like I'm still wearing a lawyer's hat. As you will understand, years of practicing law cannot be erased with a snap of my fingers because I'm in the diplomatic arena now. I'm not sure I'm explaining myself very clearly."

"I know precisely how you feel, and how and why you have come to where you are now. For that reason I feel a special affection towards you, Gabriel. You remind me a lot of the young lawyer I once was … the reasons why I was led to a second career in diplomacy are not unlike yours. The difference lies in the circumstances; mine, a brutal dictatorship, yours, the rampant corruption of our justice system."

"I'm glad you understand me. But that's not all."

"Let's see, why don't you explain it? Maybe I can help you," said Don Emilio, sipping wine from his glass. Don Emilio was one of the pillars of Dominican diplomacy. He had faced long periods of political turmoil during his diplomatic career, along with the nation he represented.

"I feel like we're up against a wall. In the sea of diplomacy, as in any other sea, the bigger fish eat the smaller ones, and smaller countries like ours are subject to the powerful ones, who dictate the parameters for how we behave. Excuse me, Don Emilio, I don't want to cause you a heart attack with what I'm going to say. But honestly, I'm losing my faith in diplomacy. I'm seeing that the principles of non-interference, of national sovereignty, only work for the powerful."

Suddenly, Gabriel fell silent. He breathed with difficulty, feeling that all the air had gone out of the cozy living room of Don Emilio's house. He looked into his host's eyes, and he saw the Ambassador, His Excellency, straighten himself up in his armchair with the authority that characterized him, looking as if he were getting ready to put Gabriel in his place. Gabriel stood up to leave, wanting to save himself the embarrassment of being called impertinent because he didn't know his limits. Who in the hell did he think he was?

"Excuse me, Your Excellency. Knowing how chivalrous you are, you'll attribute my rudeness to the wine. I wish you a good evening, and please accept my heartfelt apologies."

"Sit down, Gabriel. Let me go for some more wine; this conversation is going to be a long one."

Don Emilio returned in a few moments with a bottle, filled both glasses with wine, sat down again in his armchair, and grinning broadly, lifted his glass as if to toast the occasion.

"Where were we?" asked Don Emilio with an inviting tone of complicity and a twinkle of mischief.

"I was talking about the double standard I'm seeing with these international organizations. I was referring to the investigation into the working conditions of Haitians in our sugar industry, led by the Special Delegation of the Inter-American Commission on Human Rights, conditions which obviously should be improved, but that are not exclusive to Haitians. The irony is that the Haitian sugar industry operated under the same conditions during the U.S. interventions in Haiti in 1914 and then here in the Dominican Republic in 1916. I imagine the Commission of Investigators, while delving into the history of all this, came to the conclusion that the conditions of those times were not those of slavery. In my opinion, this noise about human rights violations, which supposedly now override the constitutional rights of a sovereign state according to the criteria of the Commission, is nothing more than a smokescreen to hide the real reasons for preventing the migration of the "boat people," as they call the Haitians who migrated here in boats, who according to their statements were "endangering the region." Human rights? The

U.S. has a long list of sins. What about the Native Americans' human rights? They were stripped of their lands and are now living on reservations that isolate them and force them to face unimaginable poverty. What about the child laborers working in the U.S.-promoted free zones of Haiti and other countries of the region? What about the mass deportations of Mexicans carried out under the principles of sovereignty and rule of law, where a nation has the right to expel anyone violating its laws? None of these international organizations speak of the human rights of Mexicans when raids or deportations are carried out, and nobody goes to Vatican City with false allegations of human rights abuses and violations. I wonder why they don't prepare a report on all the help the Dominican Republic gives to Haiti, how Dominican schools and universities are filled with Haitian students who are welcomed and assimilated by the Dominican student population without complaint and do not have the problems the "dreamers" have in the United States. No, that is never mentioned. Why not? Because they know very well that immigration problems are not exclusive to this island, but are a global matter; therefore, nations whose governments are affected with this problem have to do whatever is necessary to defend their sovereignty and their economy through their constitutions and their internal laws."

Gabriel rose to his feet as if he were on the stand defending a client. He spoke vehemently, releasing the emotions that clamped his chest like a vise. When he finished, he sat back down in his armchair opposite Don Emilio, deflated. He focused on the details of the Persian rug under his feet. He felt ashamed of his outburst and wondered if Don Emilio thought he was drunk.

"Gabriel, I wish Sandra had heard this. She'd be as proud of you as I am." Don Emilio gave his former pupil a kindly smile. He had not been mistaken as to Gabriel's human qualities. The intellectuals always stood apart.

****

7

Whenever the official agenda allowed him time to do so, Don Emilio invited Gabriel to dine at his home and discuss his former pupil's intellectual and personal concerns. Don Emilio and Doña Sandra's living room became the sanctuary where Gabriel could freely express his feelings and opinions without fear of being crucified in his fledgling diplomatic career.

They talked about diplomacy, domestic and international politics, and above all, the noble ideals that led them both into public service as diplomats.

They frequently talked about current Dominican-Haitian relations and their geopolitical relevance. Don Emilio felt rejuvenated and refreshed by the conversations he had with Gabriel, while the latter felt strengthened and encouraged by his mentor's support and understanding. Their discussions were so lively and enjoyable that Doña Sandra ended up participating in them as well. She affectionately dubbed them "the Musketeers' meetings."

"The earthquake in Haiti has given birth to a new kind of diplomacy of solidarity on the island," Gabriel noted, analyzing the current situation. "We need to focus on building pragmatic relationships between Haiti and the Dominican Republic at the grassroots level and have a broader involvement of all the sectors of the economy, if we want relations between the two countries to improve."

"You know, I still remember how impressive your research work was when you presented it in your first geopolitics class with me at the university," Don Emilio commented with satisfaction. "From that moment I knew you'd have a great future in that field, so I took a special interest in you."

"I am honored, Don Emilio. You can't imagine how much I enjoyed your classes, your anecdotes. Since then, you have been the example I've always tried to follow. You are such a well-rounded, dignified man; a true master of diplomacy."

"You're starting to make me wonder if you are saying goodbye," said Doña Sandra with a sadness in her voice, searching the faces of her husband and Gabriel to determine if what she sensed was true.

"That's right, darling," Don Emilio replied slowly and carefully. "Gabriel will be gone for a year, at least."

"Has he been assigned to a diplomatic mission somewhere?"

"No, Doña Sandra. I decided to take a sabbatical," Gabriel clarified to his hostess. "I need to know what path I'm really called to follow in my life. This experience may help me find some answers and will help me grow and mature personally and professionally. I feel that taking a year off will put me where God needs me to go."

Doña Sandra paused for a long moment before she replied. "If that's what you have to do, then may God take care of you and protect you." She approached him and gave him a motherly hug. "I'm going to miss you very much. Come back quickly and safely so that the 'Musketeers' can keep holding our meetings. I'll leave you and Don Emilio to it so you two can say goodbye." She walked quietly down the hall that led to her bedroom.

"If I had your youth, I'd go with you," Don Emilio chuckled from his armchair, trying to hide the melancholy that had created a knot in his heart when his wife had said goodbye to Gabriel.

"Thank you for your support, Don Emilio. Thank you for motivating me, for driving me to grow, to look for new horizons and new ways of looking at things in this art and science that you know so well." Gabriel stood up very quickly, feeling that if he stayed a minute longer he would break down and completely embarrass himself.

Don Emilio rose to his feet almost as quickly. He approached Gabriel and enfolded him in a bear hug, coming away with tears in his eyes. With the wisdom that only experience can give, he blessed Gabriel as his wife had done a few minutes earlier.

"Yes ... may God take care of you and protect you. And keep in mind that you are not alone in this adventure, you'll have your Sancho Panza with you in spirit." He pointed to himself and smiled.

Gabriel smiled back at his mentor, fighting back tears. "You've read my mind, Don Emilio. I feel like Quixote, tilting at windmills ... but I've got to do this."

****

8

Matilde came to her house at about eight o'clock in the evening. She had come home at that hour for months. Her workdays seemed endless. She pushed the door open, her feet dragging across the floor with fatigue, and collapsed in the nearest rocking chair in the living room. She started to cry, clutching her purse in her lap.

"Tell me, Lord, that this is just a really bad dream. I don't feel like I can take it any longer; the situation never seems to improve. In 18 months, the only thing that's changed is the date. We still keep getting waves of sick and displaced Haitians. We just don't know what to do with them any more. Those poor people ... Have mercy on them, and on us ..."

"Mom?" Gabriel, Matilde's son, flipped the light on in the darkened living room,

"Oh, holy Mother of God! You scared me to death, Gabriel! When did you come in?" Matilde wiped her tears away with her fingers and dissembled a smile, not wanting her son to see her so undone. She had always been the rock of the household.

"I came in a few minutes ago, Mom." Gabriel approached his mother and bent down to hug her, then stood back a bit, gazing at her speculatively. "You don't look well, Mom. If you keep working nonstop like this, you're going to get sick."

"I know, but ... " Matilde sighed and leaned back in the rocking chair. She couldn't get the rest of the sentence out of her mouth.

"The good thing is that I'm here, and that changes your agenda, which is something you need," Gabriel grinned. "I came home because I needed it too. It's overwhelming, this wave of immigrants coming into the country."

"So just like that, on a Wednesday evening, you decided to jump into the devil's kettle, coming back to this godforsaken town that's more like a Haitian province now ... You don't fool me. What are you up to?" Matilde narrowed her eyes, scrutinizing her son.

"I'll tell you over dinner; I'm starving. And I'm taking care of dinner because you've had to work too much already." Gabriel extended his hand to his mother to help her out of the rocking chair. They walked down the hall to the kitchen, Gabriel's right arm around Matilde's shoulders.

Gabriel puttered about the kitchen, putting together a quick dinner together for the two of them with what was on hand. A few minutes later, he ceremoniously placed a dish of boiled plantain with slices of avocado and cheese in front of Matilde, smiling down at her. "This is pretty good for a bachelor, don't you think? Or were you thinking I didn't have enough kitchen skills to get a wife?" Gabriel joked.

"Well, honestly, it's time for you to get serious about it, because if you don't, you'll become an *un*eligible bachelor." Matilde burst out laughing. Of course, she didn't believe such a thing. Her son had always been a catch, with girls fighting over him since his childhood.

"Ah! You mothers are always dreaming about grandchildren. I promise you they'll come in due time."

"Uh-huh ... We'll see about that! By the way, what are you planning? What were you going to tell me?"

Gabriel rested his fork on the edge of his plate and clasped his hands as if to pray. He sought the right words, pondering the best way to break the news and especially, express his true feelings to his mother. He cleared his throat and looked into her eyes.

"I've decided to take a sabbatical. A year off to decide what I'm going to do with the rest of my life."

Matilde put her hand over her mouth, trying to contain her astonishment at the news.

"Please, Mom, don't be alarmed. I haven't gone crazy. I've been thinking a lot about the situation in this country and about its future; and it's going to be a very gloomy one if we 'don't make some serious changes here in the Dominican Republic. I don't like anything I see. And I'm not going to stand idly by, doing nothing."

"And just what do you plan on doing?" Matilde could hardly manage to get her words out. She would never have imagined what she had just heard. She had always assumed her son would have a bright future as a high-ranking official within the legal system, or with the state department ... what was the point of getting so many postgraduate degrees?

"We need real leaders here, Mom; honest people in public service, people who can inspire and move the population. We've had enough of corruption."

Gabriel could feel the confusion in Matilde's silence, in her gaze. The pain that he had just caused her. Her disappointment, her broken dreams about her only son's future were palpable. Gabriel felt as if a dagger had sunk into his heart.

"Did you become a Communist?" asked Matilde in a tiny thread of a voice.

"Mom, what a question! Come on, you're thinking like someone from the fifties."

"I don't want the authorities labeling you as a troublemaker or worse, hunting you down ... and killing you! It's always been like that, believe me. It's not old-people stuff!"

"I didn't mean to upset you, Mom. I'm sorry. You can rest easy, I promise I'm not a Communist, nor am I involved in subversive activities or anything that would jeopardize my safety, or my family's. With regard to my job, don't worry. I've been talking with Ambassador Martínez Durán. He told me the door would always be open for me to come back whenever I was ready, and he would miss me, but he understood my position, and in fact, he applauded it and gave me his blessing."

"But, really, what do you plan to do?"

"Go to Haiti."

"Haiti? But over there, things are still the same as they were the day of the earthquake, even though it happened a year and a half ago. I don't understand!" Matilde pushed her plate away.

"I plan on immersing myself in their reality, serving in whatever capacity will be useful. I feel it's the only way to understand what's going on and find good, workable solutions to the problems affecting both Haiti and the Dominican Republic. Haiti is the other side of the coin. Or, as some poets and politicians like to say, the other wing of the bird that is Hispaniola."

Gabriel began busying himself with cleaning up the table and the kitchen. Matilde still sat at the table, immobile. The fatigue of the day and the shock of Gabriel's news left her with no strength. After a long time, she stood up with much difficulty, said good night to him, and went to her bedroom, where she sat down hard on the edge of her bed and fell back on the mattress.

****

Gabriel barely slept, mortified by the pain he had caused his mother, yet also full of excitement over what his life would bring him within a few hours. So he got up early, brewed some strong coffee, and patiently waited for Matilde to come to the kitchen. At no sign of his mother, he began to worry and went to her bedroom. He needed to talk to her before she left for work at the hospital.

"Mom, may I come in?" Gabriel said at the door of Matilde's room. "I know you're getting ready to go to work."

After a lengthy pause, Matilde opened the door. She looked completely undone, as if a bulldozer had rolled over her.

"I've got to say goodbye now, Mom, but above all, I need your blessing. I'm going to need that more than anything. Don't stop praying for me, and keep entrusting me to the Blessed Mother and the saints."

"I didn't know you'd leave so soon!" The color fled from Matilde's face at the news. She looked waxen.

"The sooner, the better. I'm going to take advantage of the fact that today is market day to cross over to Haiti."

"No, no, no!" Matilde protested with tears in her eyes. "Tell me it's not true; tell me you aren't going to go into Haiti without papers."

"I confess I've thought about it. But no, I couldn't do it that way, I can't go against my principles or my career. Rest assured I won't do anything that would compromise my safety or integrity. I'll be careful."

Gabriel approached his mother and gave her a long hug. Then he stepped back and stretched out his arms, placing his hands on Matilde's shoulders. He shared the details of his plans with her in a soft, clear voice, just as she once did with him when he was a boy.

"I have a visa to be there for one year doing an assessment study of humanitarian organizations with a presence in Haiti, measuring their performance two years after the earthquake."

All Matilde could do was burst into tears like a child.

****

9

Gabriel loaded only a few essentials into a backpack. If he was to personally experience how the Haitian people were living, he would have to do without a lot of things and live in a situation of lack, just as they did. He left Matilde's house and used a bus service to get to the Jimaní-Malpasse border crossing, located 60 kilometers from Port-au-Prince and where 80% of Dominican exports to Haiti were sold.

He arrived at the border at eight o'clock in the morning, just in time for the opening of the border gate. As soon as the gate was opened, an avalanche of about 1,500 Haitians poured through to the Dominican side, chaotically shoving and jostling in an effort to be the first to arrive at the dusty area in Jimaní set aside for the market. They were bringing whatever wares they had to sell in their arms, on their heads, or in wheelbarrows. All were vying to set themselves up in one of the vans that had been left there for their use, or on rickety folding tables, or on the ground.

The bustle was deafening. The confusion of merchants packed together like sardines in unsanitary conditions, shouting over one another in different languages, mingled with a host of pungent smells and jarring noises, and the frenzied exchange of currencies and solicitations for lodging and transportation services were beyond overwhelming. Traders from both countries were determined to make a tidy profit from the sales of their products and services, any way they could. The environment was conducive to illegal activities such as black market trading of items banned by the Haitian government and the smuggling of Haitian immigrants to the Dominican side of the border.

All this confirmed what Gabriel had already known, that Haitians were coming into Dominican territory without immigration control, and that the products being sold on the border lacked customs and quality control. A few members of the specialized Border Security Corps were posted in the area, but they casually observed the chaos like indulgent parents.

As soon as Gabriel absorbed the mental shock his border experience had given him, he stepped into the crowd and passed through the massive gate into Haitian territory. He knew he wouldn't be required to present any documents due to the complete lack of security at the border, but apprehension filled him and drops of cold sweat ran down his forehead and body just the same.

He walked at a quick pace until he felt he was a prudent distance away from the border. As he looked back to confirm how far away he was, he heard the driver of a white pickup truck announcing that he would soon be departing to Port-au-Prince. Gabriel saw that the bed of the pickup truck was packed, but jumped in without thinking twice to join the human pyramid that balanced itself precariously in the back of the vehicle.

****

As the pickup journeyed to Port-au-Prince, Gabriel alternated between sadness, discouragement, and indignation at the sight of many dozens of women and children standing along the sides of the road with cans and empty boxes or outstretched hands, begging everyone who passed by for food or money. A crushing feeling of oppression began to grow in his chest. The mountains of rubble bore witness to Haiti's total devastation and almost non-existent recovery. It seemed as if the earthquake had just happened, or that the Haitian capital had just been bombed. The presence of the United Nations blue helmets lent the impression of a city in wartime.

The many images Gabriel had seen on the news and in the press did not come close to portraying or describing the sense of helplessness in the presence of such utter desolation. At that moment, Gabriel thought he was beginning to understand the inexplicable attitude of the Haitian president after the earthquake. His ineffective response to the circumstances, which had been harshly criticized by all, was perhaps not indifference or apathy. Perhaps the sheer magnitude of what happened had left him a mere shell, without a heart, mind, or soul.

Gabriel stopped before what was left of the Cathedral of Our Lady of the Assumption in Port-au-Prince. He sat on the steps in the shadow of the cathedral's façade with its rose window, feeling as if he were a lost child. He felt emotionally undone. A blind man stood on the steps nearby, playing a guitar and singing. The melancholic chords and lyrics of the song rent Gabriel's soul.

Welcome, welcome, you who visit Haiti / You who visit my country / I bid you welcome / The leaders of Haiti are very bad /They turn a blind eye to the unfortunate/who must beg for charity / Welcome... welcome... you who visit Haiti...

With this song, Gabriel received the first of the life lessons he was seeking on this journey: the resilience of the Haitian people who have succeeded in transcending their misery and suffering. He stood up to walk toward the National Palace, passing by an evangelical pastor who shouted words of praise to God, echoed by his congregation.

Despite all the help promised to Haiti, many months after the earthquake the National Palace was still a pile of rubble and thousands of the displaced were living in the square on the Champ de Mars in precarious shelters made of whatever materials they were able to gather.

The conditions were horrific; far worse than in the poorest corners of Little Haiti in Santo Domingo, or in any other Haitian community in the Dominican Republic. The difference was that this was their country. Gabriel understood that ever since the earthquake, Haiti had been suspended in a macabre limbo, stripped of its past and future, and because of this predicament, the political, social, and economic climate on the island was extremely vulnerable.

****

Gabriel headed to where he would live, a modest hotel in downtown Port-au-Prince called the Royal Inn, recommended by some humanitarian aid representatives he'd spoken with a few months before deciding to come to Haiti.

He unpacked his backpack and remained in his room until lunchtime. He had agreed with Marcel Vincent to meet at the hotel's restaurant. Marcel would be his "host" in Haiti, the term used in diplomatic circles for the person who served as your guide during the first few days of your visit to a foreign country.

At 12:45 p.m. on the dot, Marcel Vincent came into the restaurant and greeted Gabriel, who was already waiting for him. Marcel was dark-skinned, tall and stocky, with graying hair. He was quite extroverted and jovial, with a jolly countenance thanks to a round face, a pair of sparkling dark eyes, and a smile that appeared permanently drawn on his lips. They ordered some 'sanduches,' and as they dined, made small talk to get to know each other.

"My friend Victor told me you'd be in Haiti for a while and that you needed my help to show you our country. So, what do you want to know about Haiti?" Marcel, speaking perfect Spanish, asked Gabriel in a plainspoken, forthright way as if he were a fellow member of the diaspora.

"Everything!" exclaimed Gabriel with enthusiasm, "I mean, everything that would help me understand why Haiti is how it is; what has happened to all the humanitarian aid that was offered; and what Haiti has done with that help, if it ever received it."

"Are you working for some type of secret or intelligence service?" Marcel's tone suddenly dropped a few decibels, and he looked over his shoulder to make sure no one had heard him.

"No, not at all. I'm doing a study of the Haitian reality after the earthquake. As you can probably tell, I have my theories and the information I've gathered from the press, books, and reports from the government and international organizations. But I want to see for myself whether all that information is true."

"Ah! Yes, yes. Now I remember from my talk with Victor that I'd be dealing with a philosopher-artist."

"I didn't know I was referred to like that."

"Well, Victor didn't describe you that way exactly. I figured it out when Victor told me I'd be helping the younger version of himself."

They both laughed. Indeed, Gabriel had a good bit in common with Victor Lazard, resembling the Haitian artist in his habits, attitude, and take on life. They had met in 2008 in the Colonial Zone of Santo Domingo where Lazard was exhibiting some of his works in a joint show with Enrique Valverde de la Roca, the Dominican painter and writer living in Madrid who had invited him to the country. Since then, Gabriel had maintained friendships with both men.

"What happened to the 11 billion dollars that have been donated thus far for the reconstruction of Haiti?"

"A fallacy! Half-truths published by the press. Do you want the short version of what happened to it, or the long version?" said Marcel sarcastically.

"I'll leave it to your discretion. I hope my question hasn't thrown salt on an open wound."

"Don't worry about it. In a nutshell, the world and the Haitian government weren't told that international public and private organizations in Haiti would be the recipients of the funds, or that they'd be paid out over a period of five years. The Interim Commission for the Reconstruction of Haiti did not approve any projects that had been submitted for approval because vested interests didn't agree on anything. I hope you can read between the lines from there, because I don't want to mention the names of any prominent international political figures, specific countries, or any international or Haitian organizations. The point is that everyone wanted to impose their own agenda and lobbied for their own interests, completely ignoring the displaced and the mountains of rubble that buried Port-au-Prince, which bury it still."

As Marcel spoke, his face turned shadowy and grave. He narrated the movie playing in his mind as he flipped over his paper napkin in agitation and rolled it between his thumb and forefinger. When he finished talking, he grabbed it with his left hand and crumpled it into a ball.

"It's a pity the international community, or those who represented it, behaved like that in the face of the Haitian people's pain. I want to believe the sheer magnitude of the tragedy was what caused the lack of adequate, effective and prompt solutions and that they had no choice but to wing it. I agree with you that without attending to priorities, any reconstruction work was going to be like trying to build a house from the roof down," Gabriel commented.

"True. Unfortunately, we've got other problems to add to it, like the government's corruption and inability to operate, even now. As a matter of fact, everything is aimed at maintaining the status quo to capitalize on our misery and reap the benefits of external financing from transnational non-governmental organizations. If you want, I can show you what has been achieved in that regard. You won't believe it! Let's go to the Market first, which is the only place that has been cleared of rubble, and I can show you the few houses that have been built so far. Building new homes for the displaced in Port-au-Prince has been very difficult due to the dysfunctional real estate system we have. Render unto Caesar that which belongs to Caesar," muttered Marcel.

"What do you mean?"

"We have a system like the one that was prevalent in medieval Europe. We have a dual system divided between lineage property obtained by inheritance, and acquired property that is simply purchased. It isn't easy to determine which parcels are lineage property, and which are acquired."

"So acquired properties can be disposed of by their owners however and whenever they want to."

"Correct, but lineage property cannot be sold because it never leaves the family line. Ownership of lineage property is more like a right to use the land. The property passes into the hands of the next couple who marries, but goes back to the family line if one of them dies. And to complicate things, if a family member leaves the land, the property rights remain dormant. Imagine the chaos with so many people missing after the earthquake. So in the area where houses for the displaced were supposed to be built, a whole lot of people claimed to have either acquired property rights and or lineage property rights, and there was no way to prove anything. Can you imagine the pandemonium?"

From his studies, Gabriel recalled the chaos that had pervaded the real estate system in the Dominican Republic before the Torrens System was introduced during the first U.S. military occupation through Executive Order 511 of June 21, 1920.

"Let's go," said Gabriel, filled with curiosity. He leaped up from his seat to follow Marcel out the hotel's entrance.

****

11

From the passenger seat of the grey 2007 Toyota Camry Marcel was driving, Gabriel confirmed what his host had described. The exorbitant sums of money donated for Haiti's reconstruction had vanished behind the smokescreen of humanitarian aid. He realized that no other foreigners were in Haiti except for international aid workers and the blue helmets of MINUSTAH. Who was Marcel? Gabriel wondered as he listened to his host.

"Marcel, how do you know things that are obviously not public?" asked Gabriel. He was shocked that Marcel knew about the tensions within the Interim Commission for the Reconstruction of Haiti, the transnational non-governmental organizations, and the ineffectiveness of the Haitian government. "You speak with the authority of a diplomat or government representative and you seem to be quite well-informed about how the humanitarian aid is being handled."

"Well, we say in Haiti that 'if you stay around honey, something's going to stick to you,'" laughed Marcel. "Let's say it's a quirk of our culture."

"Marcel, Dominicans are known for that too. Nobody is ever surprised when confidential government information gets leaked to the public." Gabriel laughed too, but then fell quiet, lost in his thoughts. Marcel brought him back to reality.

"Going back to the subject of humanitarian aid and the reconstruction of Haiti, you'll see these matters are without head or tail, like the saying goes. It's a very sad chapter of our recent history. As I was telling you, this party was set up by the international community and sponsored by NGOs and private economic interests, and Haiti was not invited to the party."

"Do you think it was because only 30% of government officials survived the earthquake?"

"No. It is due to the fact that charity is a very lucrative business, so much so that according to reports from the U.S. State Department, after the earthquake, no fewer than 10,000 transnational non-governmental organizations were operating here. Haiti has become a playground for organizations to operate without any government control and on top of that, benefit from tax exemptions. Nor were they ever transparent regarding how most of that humanitarian aid was used. Did you know that the many millions of dollars donated to Haiti by U.S. citizens were used to pay for the deployment and maintenance of U.S. troops here? Over 200 million dollars!"

"An atrocity!"

"Yes, but if you look carefully, you'll see that it's really just the same atrocity that isolated my country when it became independent. Back then, we were being isolated to prevent abolitionist ideas from spreading and affecting the economies of powerful countries. Now, we're being isolated to preserve the gains being made by vested interests off of Haiti's misfortune."

"Based on what you're telling me, it seems like a real international and national conspiracy."

"I won't disagree with that. It's the truth, indeed. What we've talked about only scratches the surface of the Haitian reality. We're talking about institutionalized corruption in Haiti. Um, it's getting dark, I'd better get you back to the hotel before nightfall. I strongly recommend that you not leave the hotel at night. You do not want to expose yourself to unnecessary dangers."

"Got it."

Gabriel got out of Marcel's Camry at the hotel entrance and went straight to his room.

****

12

Gabriel paced back and forth in front of the colonial-style bed in his room. He wanted to clarify his thoughts. He was upset mentally, emotionally, and physically. The hunger pangs and growling from his empty stomach distracted him. Yet every time he moved toward the door to go to the restaurant for dinner, he lost his appetite again. Guilt consumed him. He realized his experience in Haiti would be a farce if he was living it from the comfort of a hotel room. He thought out loud, asking God for guidance.

God, what is Your will for me? What do you want me to do? I thought I knew ... but I'm not sure anymore. All I know is I can't go on with this anguish in my heart. Give me wisdom to discern what I must do, the good sense to know how to get started, and the strength to get where I need to go.

He sat in the armchair to meditate. He concentrated on slowing his breathing, and meditated for half an hour. When he finished, he felt at peace. He grabbed his mobile phone, and heard himself communicate his plans with assertiveness.

"Mom, I hope I didn't disturb you," Gabriel said as soon as he heard Matilde's tired voice.

"How can you say such things, son? Thank God you called me. Where are you? How are you? I feel like I'm dying of anguish; how am I going to handle this? And you only just left."

"Mom, it's all right. I'm already in Port-au-Prince. I'm at the Royal Inn. But after tomorrow, I don't know where I'll be."

"How can you do not know?"

"I just changed my plans. I was going to stay here, but it won't be like that anymore."

I will work wherever I'm needed, so I won't be in contact as frequently I thought I'd be. Don't worry about me, and don't start imagining the worst; I'm going to be okay. Calm down. Where is your faith?" Mercedes had been weeping but fell silent. She was crying on the inside, and Gabriel knew it.

****

After breakfast, Gabriel went to the reception desk. He reported that he was being required in another city, so he would be absent for a few days. He stayed in the reception area where he had told Marcel to meet him. As agreed, at half-past nine, Marcel came to the hotel.

"Good morning, Gabriel." Marcel gripped Gabriel's hand with enthusiasm. "Tell me, where are we going today?"

"Marcel, I want you to take me where I can stay doing volunteer work."

"Did I understand you correctly? Are you leaving the hotel? I'm confused … "

"Yes, that's what I want to do. Participate in the reconstruction of your country." Gabriel looked directly into Marcel's eyes.

"I'm amazed, really. How do you want to do that?"

"I told you yesterday when we met. I need to understand the reality of your country."

"And what are you looking for? I don't understand."

"I'm seeking a purpose." Gabriel began walking to the hotel entrance in long, quick strides, and Marcel struggled to keep up with him due to his weight.

"A purpose?" Marcel echoed in disbelief when he caught up with Gabriel in front of his Toyota Camry. He stared at Gabriel for a long moment, wanting to understand him.

"I'm seeking the purpose of my life ..."

****

13

After talking with Gabriel about what he wanted to do in Haiti, Marcel put him in touch with a group of people he felt would benefit greatly from the help Gabriel was willing to offer. These people were dedicated to improving the lives of the Haitian children called *restaveks*.

"I think you will find what you're looking for right here," said Marcel, turning off the ignition and removing the key. "You are going to be able to help improve one of the biggest problems my country has, which will worsen due to a sharp increase in our birth rate since the earthquake, bringing more children into the world. If there were about 300,000 boys and girls living in a terrible situation before the earthquake, now there are many more, and that number will continue to grow."

"What do you mean?"

"I am referring to the *restaveks*. Children placed with relatives, neighbors, or strangers to take care of them and provide them with the education and better living conditions their biological parents cannot give them due to poverty. These are Haiti's new slaves, Gabriel. I guess you know about this matter. Being a lawyer, I am sure you'd like to work to help eliminate child labor and child abuse."

"Of course. I know they are forced to work without stopping, that they are often physically and sexually abused. What can I do for them here?"

"You can use your talents, your strong convictions, your powers of persuasion to create a change in the way mothers think, to make them understand that this system of the *restaveks* is a heinous scheme. Let's go in; I'll introduce you to some of the coordinators of the campaign against this type of child abuse and exploitation."

"Marcel, how nice to see you! What brings you here?" Antoine Philippe, a man of medium height and clear complexion, the director of the center where the *restaveks* were taken in, extended his hand to Marcel in greeting.

"I want to introduce you to Gabriel Novoa Ramírez, who wants to volunteer for this organization."

"Very nice to meet you." Gabriel shook Antoine's hand.

"Gabriel will spend a whole year in Haiti doing a study on our reality since the earthquake. I told him this would be the best place to kill two birds with one stone. Here, I think he will get the information he is looking for, while you will have his help. It will be a win-win situation!" Marcel announced with his characteristic laughter. Everyone joined him.

"Yes, I'm willing to help in whatever capacity I'm needed," interjected Gabriel with enthusiasm.

"Well, you can start working with us here in Port-au-Prince or in some of the rural communities. If you decide to stay in the capital, you can help us directly with the children who come to the center. If you decide to go to the rural areas, you can help us with the mothers, explaining the dangers their sons and daughters are exposed to if they are sent to live in the capital."

"Marcel and I had already discussed the second option. I think I could start out there to familiarize myself with the country, the situation of these minors while I get the information I need for the study I'm doing at the same time. Then I could come back to help you in Port-au-Prince."

"Then no more needs to be said," replied Antoine with excitement. "Gabriel, you will help us in the community of Petit-Goave to raise awareness among the mothers, because they are the head of the household in Haiti, so they do not send their children to Port-au-Prince as *restaveks*; to let them know that these children will not be taken care of but will be forced to work as slaves."

Gabriel joined a group of ten people in charge of visiting rural communities to warn mothers of the life their children would have if they sent them to the capital for what they thought would be a better life. The campaign was simple; they merely spoke with whoever was interested in listening to them while passing out flyers illustrating the hardships the *restaveks* faced with stark images and words.

With enthusiasm and a mysterious sense of mission, Gabriel spoke with two or three people at a time at first, but soon the number of participants grew so that the talks had to be held in larger improvised areas that were normally used as community meeting places. He expressed himself in prefect Creole, to the surprise of his teammates and the inhabitants of the poor communities they visited.

"The *restaveks* work from sunup to sundown without payment or any kind of compensation. Your children are better off by your side. Don't look at your sons and daughters as a burden, and don't think you won't be able to keep them," Gabriel urged, addressing a group of eight women. "You send them with someone to the capital in the hope they'll have the life you cannot give them; you expect they'll provide them with food, clothing and an education. But quite the opposite happens; in these places your sons and daughters will be malnourished, and will lack the clothing and formal education that drive you to give them away. They will be physically and sexually abused; they will suffer daily humiliation, and will face constant stress and anxiety. Keep your sons and daughters with you; don't allow them to be enslaved; don't reduce them to nothing because you think you have nothing to offer them. As mothers, you have the most important thing you can give them, which is your love, your support and your guidance, so that they can grow up safe and confident. Let's end this practice that leaves them with no hope, no future, and no dignity."

When Gabriel finished speaking, the voices of the mothers rose in great waves, washing over him and Marie Thérèse, the volunteer in charge of illustrating the flyers. Some mothers asked how to rescue the sons and daughters they had given away; others thanked the spirits because they had saved the offspring who were about to be plucked from them from certain misfortune.

"You have a way with people," noted Marie Thérèse. "You're persuasive, and there is a vehemence in your speech. I enjoy listening to you."

"Seeing the reaction of the mothers when they learn the truth about the trap of the *restaveks* really motivates me. I always ask God for help in raising awareness about this modern-day child slavery."

"I believe God has heard your prayers." Marie Thérèse's face shone. She had felt a great admiration and attraction to Gabriel since she met him for the first time as his teammate.

"Thanks and praise be to God," commented Gabriel, who without noticing Marie Thérèse's subtle flirting, stooped to gather up the flyers the mothers had left on the ground.

****

14

Marie Thérèse Cadet was a young dark-skinned Haitian professional. She had a slender figure and elegant bearing, striking black eyes, a sensual mouth and oval face perfectly framed by her pixie haircut. She was a very dynamic woman. She had returned from Montreal, Canada after the earthquake, as most Haitians from the diaspora had returned to their homeland to selflessly assist, first with the rescue of victims, and then with the reconstruction of Haiti.

She, like Gabriel, enjoyed research and had excellent language skills, enabling her to present ideas in an attractive and innovative way. Ever since Gabriel had joined the cause against the practice of the *restaveks*, Marie Thérèse had enjoyed working with him in the fields of her country. She identified a good bit with the young volunteer whom she got to know better as the days passed, but at the same time, she found him an enigma.

"I can't believe we've been traveling around the countryside for a month to raise awareness about the plight of the *restaveks* and keeping my people from giving away their children," commented Marie Thérèse over dinner with Gabriel. They had prepared the last provisions they had brought with them, and were sharing them with some of the locals who approached the portable stove and pot.

"Unbelievable, but true. Though it seems like it's been longer than that to me," Gabriel replied quietly.

"We'll return to Port-au-Prince tomorrow, so you can start working with the kids at the center, if you want. It occurred to me that you could start teaching them how to read and write; you speak French and Creole fluently. You could practically pass for someone from the Haitian diaspora, like me."

"For the record, I've never intended to deceive anyone. I am one hundred percent pure Dominican."

"Sorry. I didn't mean it that way. I was giving you a compliment, really."

"A compliment? How?"

"Well, since I came here from Montreal after the earthquake, I've met many Dominicans who've helped us out here. Many are still coming, most of them doctors, who spend a week or two volunteering here, and then they go back to the Dominican Republic. Out of all these people, I have met only one Dominican who speaks fluent French and Creole. I wanted to find out why, so I looked up your profile on social media, and found the answer I was looking for. It's because of your career as a diplomat."

"Keep in mind, Marie Thérèse, that curiosity killed the cat," joked Gabriel. "But, yes, that's the truth."

"Then, why are you sitting here in the middle of a field in my country, away from the pomp and circumstance of diplomacy?"

"Because I need to know Haiti more intimately, its true reality, what and who its people truly are, in order to understand and find solutions to the challenges of the Dominican reality. We share the same island; we also share big problems that will only be solved if broad-based joint measures are adopted and implemented, with a spirit of solidarity."

"I agree with you on that. But I sense there's more to it than that ... isn't there?"

"Believe me, if I tell you the truth, you're going to declare me a *persona non grata*." Gabriel rose from the piece of cardboard on the ground that had served as a seat. He wanted to avoid what he felt would be inevitable: a confrontation with Marie Thérèse.

"Gabriel, wait. I think I know."

"I promise I'll tell you and we'll talk about it in Port-au-Prince."

Gabriel knew that once his friend discovered the truth, she would see him as another Brutus: a traitor and a conspirator.

****

15

Once they had returned to Port-au-Prince, Gabriel went to the Royal Inn, where he had previously stayed. The receptionist was glad to see him, to have a familiar face back at the hotel. He managed the little hotel waiting every day for the miracle to come that would bring business back to normal. The earthquake had also killed Haiti's tourism. The only foreigners who were interested in Haiti now were the international aid volunteers and the MINUSTAH blue helmets; the novelty of Haiti's misfortune had vanished with time.

Gabriel showered and changed clothes in his room, thinking about what he needed to do next. He was trying to think up a good excuse to give Antoine Philippe so he could stay away from the center in case Marie Thérèse did not understand the reasons for his actions and the atmosphere at the center became hostile. He pondered whether it might be better if he went to another city to continue his quest about Haiti. He grabbed his cell phone and dialed Antoine's number.

"Antoine, it's Gabriel Novoa Ramirez. I just wanted to let you know I won't be at the Center tomorrow like we'd planned. I have some personal affairs to take care of. I'll be in touch as soon as they're resolved.."

"Don't worry. Do what you need to do. You're always welcome here, Gabriel. Thank you for letting me know … see you soon."

Gabriel stood there with the phone in his hand, calculating his next action like a military strategist. He dialed the next number.

"Hi, Marcel. It's Gabriel Novoa Ramírez. How are you?"

"Counting my blessings, you know, those little miracles that happen every day that go unseen by people who live in more privileged countries, but are far more noticeable and appreciated if you happen to live in Haiti. Where are you now?"

"I'm back in Port-au-Prince, at the Royal Inn again. This time, I'm in room 202. I was calling to find out your availability for tomorrow."

"Let me see ... tomorrow is Thursday ... available! What do you want to do?"

"I wanted to see if we could go to Ouanaminthe or Dajabón and check to see if this project that's been planned for years under Lomé IV was executed."

"Umm ... It'll be a fairly long road trip. We'd better take the road to Gonaïves, go through Cap-Haïtien, continue on to Ouanaminthe, and cross over to Dajabón. We'll have to leave Port-au-Prince as early as possible. How about 7:00 in the morning?"

"Okay. I'll meet you at 7:00 tomorrow morning at the hotel reception desk. Thank you, Marcel. See you tomorrow."

Gabriel sat on the edge of the bed feeling a bit more relaxed. He noticed that his phone's battery was low, and rummaged for his charger in his backpack. With the charger in his free hand, he called Matilde. Her voice mail greeting came on, asking him to leave a message.

"Hi, Mom. I'm back in Port-au-Prince at the Royal Inn, Room 202. I am good, thank God, and I hope you are too. I know you're working, but I just wanted to let you know. I'll call you later. I'm sending you a big hug. I love you very much."

Gabriel stood up and went to the console where the television was, and plugged in the charger, leaving his phone to charge. He sat down again on the edge of the bed and meditated for about thirty minutes. When he opened his eyes, he got up and grabbed the phone from the charger. He felt a slight, inexplicable fear as he dialed.

"Good afternoon, Marie Thérèse. It's Gabriel Novoa Ramírez. I'm calling to invite you to lunch, here at the hotel. Is 1:00 p.m. okay? We'll have our conversation about what's going on, like I promised. See you soon." He hung up, wishing to be brief and not go into any details.

****

Marie Thérèse and Gabriel met at the reception desk and walked together to the restaurant, where they chose a table that seemed to favor conversation, one located in a corner at the back of the restaurant.

"I'm still new in Haiti, so I have no idea where else we could have had lunch considering the circumstances. At least, I know the food is good here." Gabriel held out a chair for Marie Thérèse, then took a seat beside her. The server appeared with a basket of bread rolls. They both ordered the soup of the day, as neither of them were particularly hungry.

Marie Thérèse gazed at Gabriel with curiosity. She smiled at him, took one of the rolls, and began to gracefully butter and eat it, piece by piece.

Gabriel returned her smile. He knew that his friend was looking for a way to create a relaxed atmosphere to encourage conversation.

"I come from a humble family," Gabriel began. "I was born in Jimaní so I was exposed to Creole throughout my childhood. I love history, and I rail against injustice; I think that's why I became a lawyer. I graduated from university at a very young age. Our legal system, like the Haitian legal system, is based on the Napoleonic Code. In fact, the Dominican Republic's code is the Spanish translation of the 1804 French code. Therefore, our jurisprudence is very closely related to French jurisprudence. I studied French because of that, and above all, because I enjoyed reading the French legal works I borrowed from some of my mentors. I decided to get a master's degree in diplomatic and international services when I began to see our courts were rife with corruption. At first, I noticed just a few courts suffered from this scourge, then I realized it had taken over the entire judicial system. In my eagerness to be well prepared to take it on, I also studied political science and Dominican constitutional law. This boring, long preamble is to explain why I speak Creole and French."

"On the contrary, I find it fascinating, Gabriel. I can hardly wait for you to tell me the rest." Marie Thérèse looked as if she were preparing herself to say something else, but fell silent when the server returned to the table with the soup bowls and placed the bowls in front of them. They said "bon appétit" to one another and started to eat.

"I was working for the legal department at the Dominican chancellery, Division of Haitian Affairs, so I am well aware of the tense relationship between our two nations, which have deteriorated even further since the allegations of abuse of Haitians in the sugar industry and the forced mass repatriations of Haitians." Gabriel paused and propped his spoon against his soup bowl, looking at his guest, trying to figure out her thoughts. But Marie Thérèse appeared to be calm and very interested in what Gabriel was saying.

"And you came to Haiti because they sent you here?" asked Marie Thérèse.

"No, I'm here on my own. I took a year-long sabbatical ... I had reached a point in my career where I felt the diplomatic field was not where I should to be any more."

The server came back to remove their soup bowls and asked if they wanted anything else. Gabriel and Marie Thérèse, suddenly feeling hungry, ordered roast chicken, mashed potatoes and boiled vegetables. They both sensed their conversation was just beginning.

"I think we all go through that," Marie Thérèse noted quietly. "It happened to me, when I saw my compatriots rescuing themselves, pulling themselves out from under the rubble using their bare hands; my life changed completely when I realized we Haitians had been abandoned, left to our own fate; international rescuers were rescuing their own first. The events of those days completely erased my life in Montreal in one fell swoop. As the days went by, I felt so helpless when I saw how all the international aid ended up disappearing in the same bureaucratic rabbit holes that prevail in all international organizations. Nothing happens there but a lot of talking. Sorry about the part of it that relates to you."

"No, don't be sorry, Marie Thérèse, you're right. In my case, the trigger was the international campaign mounted to discredit the Dominican Republic every time the country, as a sovereign and independent state, applied its constitution and immigration laws against those illegally living in its territory. The irony is that there is no drama in the international community when other Caribbean states repatriate Haitians or any other country repatriates undocumented people, sending them back to their country of origin. Of course, there cannot be any drama publicly at least, because this is a matter of universal legal principles, which are not subject to interpretation by any foreign country or the international community."

Gabriel paused again, longer this time, with the intent to assess his friend's reaction. He was sure he had touched a sore spot, as he was speaking with someone from the transgressing country. He noticed that Marie Thérèse had grabbed her napkin. Gabriel thought she would interpret his words as an insult, throw the napkin in the middle of the table, and storm out in anger. But she did not. Instead, Marie Thérèse delicately touched her mouth to the napkin, laid it back on her lap, and placed her hands on the edge of the table, intertwining her fingers.

"Are you looking for the most effective way to repatriate my compatriots?"

"No, I'm looking for a way to preserve the two nations. It seems to me like it's a pie-in-the-sky ideal ... "

"Explain. I don't understand."

The waiter came back to retrieve their entrée dishes and ask if they wanted some dessert. They both ordered crème brûlée. And Gabriel went on with his explanation.

"I'm looking for ways for our two nations to coexist, as they have since they were formed, but not just simply tolerate each other as they always have in the past; I want peace, harmony, and cooperation between them. I want to prevent what powerful countries with vested interests in Haiti have been plotting internationally. They want Haiti to continue to be reduced to nothing so they can keep benefiting from it and impose their agenda on the other side of the island, in the belief that if Haitians stay on Hispaniola, they won't migrate to their countries. Yes, there are very powerful interests who want to maintain the status quo in Haiti so the Dominican Republic has to carry the weight of what the Haitian government cannot do, and what the international community ought to do but won't."

Just when Gabriel was going to elaborate on his ideas, the server appeared yet again, bringing the dessert which they both consumed in silence. Gabriel did not lift his eyes off the plate. He thought about how the server had showed up to interrupt the rhythm and course of the conversation every time he ventured into turbulent waters. Was it some type of sign?

"Thanks for the lunch and the company," Marie Thérèse said with a strange formality. She placed her napkin on the table, grabbed her purse, and stood up.

"Forgive me, Marie Thérèse, I didn't mean to offend you. Now you know why I didn't want to talk about this out in the field. If you don't want to speak to me any more after this conversation, I'll understand."

Marie Thérèse opened her mouth to say something, but no sound came out. She shook her head and left the restaurant without looking back.

****

16

Gabriel went to his room with heavy steps. Suddenly he felt an overwhelming fatigue, and a deep sadness because he thought his words had hurt Marie Thérèse. Unfortunately, there was nothing to be done. That was the price he had to pay to maintain his authenticity; the truth had to be said, even if it hurt. He dialed his mother, keeping his word that he would call her later.

"Mom, I'm glad I got you on the line. Tell me, how are you feeling, how have you been?"

"I'm fine, thank goodness. But you better tell me how you're holding up. I'm praying for you every minute of every day!"

"Thank you for your prayers, Mom. I'm fine, all things considered. It's really been a transformative experience."

"I don't doubt it, son. I've seen only a small part of Haiti's tragedy from this side of the island. I can imagine how upsetting it must be, being in the midst of it."

"Yeah, it was for a while. I'll tell you more about it later ... for now, I just want to reassure you, to let you know I'm okay, and above all, to ask for your blessing again."

"Are you hiding something from me, Gabriel? You sound weird."

"I am really tired; that's all. I love you very much."

"And I love you more. May God's blessing be with you always, and come back safe and sound."

Gabriel dropped the phone on the bed and sat on the corner of the mattress. He put his hands up to his head as if he were grabbing a ball that was about to burst. He replayed mental images of his lunch with Marie Thérèse. He began to speak aloud to himself, and to God.

I beg your forgiveness, God, for the hurt I've caused my friend. Help me to forgive myself for my actions and free me from these painful memories. I feel mortified because I couldn't tell Marie Thérèse everything I wanted to say. I felt so pressured by her possible reaction that I didn't say everything I really wanted to. I appreciate the fact that Marie Thérèse didn't make a fuss in the restaurant, but her leaving didn't give me an opportunity to explain my position on Haitian repatriations a little better; it isn't from being inflexible, and it isn't based on racism, and it's far from the chauvinism that always comes out in Dominican-Haitian relations. Yes, you know, Lord God, how we Dominicans are. We don't hesitate to defend our land when it comes to Haitians, or anybody.

I wonder how best to express the patriotism we are supposed to practice daily? When we have to defend the nation from ourselves, from impunity, from corruption, from a lack of respect for its institutions, and from the reversal of our values that is sinking our society ...

The Dominican Republic needs a change, but it won't take place unless there's a change in Haiti, because to get out of the quicksand we're both in, we need a change in our way of thinking and our cultures, a change that must be based on strong economic growth; a growing, prosperous economy brings social and political stability to both sides of the island. Only then will both wings of this bird take flight, only then will these conjoined brothers be able to walk. We've got to stop being like crabs in a bucket, all pulling each other back down into the bucket in an attempt to get out. Merciful and Almighty God, only you can save us ...

Gabriel turned the light off in his room and laid down on the bed, immersed in his monologue to God.

****

17

After listening to Gabriel, Marie Thérèse was very confused. She rushed into the hotel where she was staying. Now, her room felt like a deep well instead of the peaceful haven where she had been living since her arrival in Haiti.

Why do I feel so vulnerable? Was it because I heard a harsh truth that is an open secret? A truth I've lived and witnessed for almost two years? Am I upset because I know in my heart that Haiti has been betrayed by the world once again? What was it about our conversation that bothered me so much? Why am I feeling so restless since I heard what Gabriel had to say?

Marie Thérèse went to the bathroom and showered. She climbed into bed wearing an oversized gray T-shirt. She tossed about, unable to fall asleep. This was not new; she had been suffering from insomnia since she had arrived to volunteer. The nightmare of her initial experiences haunted her, a form of torture she faced every night before finally falling asleep. Despite the passage of time, she could still feel and hear the dread of despair, the voices and cries of her compatriots begging for help, the hands covered with blood and concrete dust trying to rescue others trapped under the rubble ... She breathed deeply and sighed, but the horror movie did not stop. It relentlessly laid bare the vulnerability of her people, the mothers going out of their minds searching for their children, the disoriented children crying for their mothers, and the heartbreaking madness many of them had descended into because they believed they were already consigned to hell, and therefore, refused to take back their children once they were found; she saw how this situation was exploited by vultures disguised as adoption agencies who took thousands of these children out of the country with summary and questionable procedures. She also saw with the victims of cholera, an epidemic that had been introduced to the country by those who came to help, and had spread like wildfire throughout the country, dealing the coup de grace to many who had managed to survive the earthquake.

Yes, Gabriel was right, Haiti was the perfect business opportunity for vested interests; it was a cash cow. Behind the façade of humanitarian aid, "non-profit" non-governmental organizations were getting rich off of Haiti's misfortune. And not to mention all the promised donations that had vanished because they were used to fund the operations and expenses of the same organizations that donated these resources, because the organizations supposedly didn't know how to distribute the aid due to the magnitude of the chaos ... and if one took a look at Port-au-Prince, Léogâne, and Cité Soleil, the incompetence or deliberate lack of interest if not the complete non-existence of the Haitian government were painfully obvious. A government deprived of almost all its institutions and officials. The few officials who survived accepted fat offers from these non-governmental organizations to come work for them and finish Haiti off. Yes, Haiti was a ghost state, and worst of all, everything indicated it would continue to be, perhaps for decades.

Marie Thérèse hugged one of the pillows as if it were a lifesaver in an ocean of sad and painful memories. She closed her eyes and invoked the protection of the spirits.

****

At nine o'clock in the morning, Marie Thérèse went to the center with a renewed determination to make a difference in the lives of the *restaveks*. It was what kept her moving forward in a country where everything remained lost in time. Boys and girls of different ages occupied two covered galleries that served as classrooms during the day.

"Good morning, Marie Thérèse, it's good to have you back at the Center," Antoine said, smiling.

"Good morning, Antoine. I'm glad to be back too; I've missed spending time with you and the rest of the volunteer staff. Don't look at me like that! You know I love the work I do in the rural areas, but I also like working with the children. I am happy knowing they're learning how to read and write at the same time they are getting help to heal from their trauma. I feel that we're changing their lives and giving them hope with what we are doing."

"Yes. We're giving them the opportunity to put themselves on the map of life and our country."

"And that personal satisfaction will be priceless for them. Yesterday I talked to Gabriel about it. He can start teaching the children today because he knows French and Creole."

"You'll want to work with Marianne on that; she has a great connection with the kids. Gabriel isn't coming today."

"What? Did he tell you why? Is he sick?" Marie Thérèse feigned surprise to hide her concerns.

"No, he's okay, thank God. He mentioned that he had personal affairs to attend to, and that he'd be in touch as soon as he was available."

Marie Thérèse felt as if someone had thrown a bucket of cold water on her. She was overwhelmed with guilt and sadness. She would have bet anything that Gabriel's absence was due to their lunch conversation going sideways.

"Umm ... That sounds like a very diplomatic way out, it sounds more like a goodbye to me. I don't think we'll be hearing from him again."

"And why do you say that? Gabriel is a responsible and genuine person who truly wants to help ..."

"Ah! Let's just say it's women's intuition, Antoine." Marie Thérèse pretended to be strong, but felt her heart falling to pieces.

****

18

Marcel and Gabriel greeted each other with a hearty handshake at the reception desk of the hotel. Marcel could hardly contain his curiosity and peppered Gabriel with questions about his experience in the countryside and the progress he was making in his research on Haiti.

"I've been thinking a lot about you," Marcel commented as they got into his Camry and drove off. "I've been wondering if I steered you in the right direction, if your experience with the *restaveks* had been useful for the research you are doing."

"Very useful, indeed. And incredibly eye-opening. I'm so grateful for what you've done for me. My experience with the *restaveks* showed me another perspective on the Haitian educational system. The number of illiterates here will continue to grow in direct proportion to the rising birth rate, unless the minorities in power realize they must invest in education to eradicate poverty and improve Haiti's quality of life. These elites must be the ones to put the pieces together of the Haitian government after the earthquake."

"You're right. Education is expensive and 85% of it is in the hands of the private sector. Before the earthquake only 50% of school-age children went to school. Public education was scarce then, and is non-existent now. The government needs to create schools and provide them with trained teachers and textbooks in order to guarantee the right to education that is established in the Haitian Constitution. We were the first nation in the Americas to pass a law on mandatory education. Quite a daring feat on the part of our ancestors at the dawn of the nineteenth century, and it's the greatest irony of our present reality, because public education does not exist. The Haitian government needs to rescue the educational system, restore the National University, and create more universities and more technical schools."

"I notice the same frustration in your voice I felt the day I met you when you gave me the nutshell summary of the state of humanitarian aid in Haiti."

"You are very observant, and you are correct. Want another nutshell summary?"

Gabriel nodded.

"It's been almost two years since the earthquake, but no schools have been built here, let alone any public ones. The earthquake intensified the privatization of education. Temporary classrooms were opened where schools vanished in the rubble and students and teachers still lie dead underneath; the structures of some of the schools that made it through the earthquake have been repaired, and some schools have been operating in pre-existing facilities that were once used for other things. But no new schools have been built at all. The National University hasn't even been repaired, and 11 of its departments are still in ruins. But thanks to the generosity of the Dominican government, in Cap-Haïtien the construction of a new university is being planned. Explain that to me! And I do not quite understand how one is supposed to teach the thousands of children living in the settlements for the displaced, where they've opened up private schools in pre-existing facilities."

"You look upset. What's bothering you?" Gabriel watched his host.

"Honestly, it chaps my hide that they want to keep us as we are. I hope the university being donated by the Dominican government will be a public one. According to the press, under the resolutions that have been adopted by international organizations, thousands upon thousands of schools are supposed to be built to provide a free quality education to all Haitian children with $250 million that the Inter-American Development Bank will disburse in 5 years, plus another $250 million more the IDB will collect from other donors. But what they *don't* say is that this aid is going to subsidize private schools so *their* students don't have to pay. And of course, they will establish a selection process to determine which schools will receive the subsidies, which will inevitably lead to discrimination and non-inclusion, not universalization, education for all. As you see, they are mere promises of help, like those made by many notable personalities who came here saying they were 'committed to helping us,' just so they could appear in the international press covering the reconstruction of Haiti. "

Marcel and Gabriel both paused, each submerged in his own world trying to absorb a truth that was very difficult to absorb and accept. For Marcel, it was the same vicious circle as ever; for Gabriel, it was the abyss into which the Dominican Republic had fallen when Haiti collapsed.

"I can almost hear the wheels of your thoughts moving. Tell me about them," Marcel encouraged, breaking the silence.

"About the millions of pesos the Dominican government is spending on the education of Haitian students, who are given this education for free by order of the Ministry of Education, just like any Dominican student, as well as free uniforms, school supplies, books, notebooks, backpacks, breakfast and a snack."

"Dominicans are carrying a good deal of the burden of our misfortune and having to deal with the consequences of the Haitian government's inability to act."

"That's right, but the saddest thing is that our cooperation and our contribution to Haiti's welfare are not recognized or appreciated internationally. Allegations of mistreatment and abuse of Haitians by Dominicans rooted in racism are always brought up by international organizations whenever the Dominican Republic executes its immigration laws. Don't you think, Marcel?"

"A volatile and controversial subject, no doubt. Even more so when ignorance is manipulated to provoke hostilities and gain a political advantage; I told you, it's very lucrative to keep us without head or tail." Marcel looked at Gabriel out of the corner of his eye, and Gabriel realized it was the second time he had deliberately used this nuanced saying.

"I disagree. To me, it does have a head and tail. But the head and tail are in the possession of those who want to keep the status quo of poverty and political weakness."

"You know, every time I talk to you I feel like I'm talking to Victor. Oh, how I miss him."

Marcel took his eyes off the road for a couple of seconds to take Gabriel's measure. He had gotten the answer he had been expecting from Gabriel about the saying "without head or tail."

"Nobody's told me whether you two are related, or what other type of tie binds you. Of course, I will respect your silence if you don't wish to reveal it."

"You are very funny," replied Marcel, laughing. "I will satisfy your curiosity by sharing with you that we are united by a bond of affection, while not by blood. Which is worth a lot."

"Of course. Even I feel like we are family," Gabriel commented, looking over at Marcel with great sincerity and a broad smile on his face. They both roared with laughter.

After nearly three hours, they arrived in the city of Gonaïves, in the department of Artibonite. They stopped there briefly to rest and stretch their legs.

"It would have been easier to reach Cap-Haïtien from the city of Santiago de los Caballeros, but I didn't mention that to you because I figured you weren't interested in seeing Santiago, you already know your country quite well. What do you expect to find over the border in Dajabón?"

"I don't know whether to laugh or cry at that question. I think *you'll* end up hating me too, for dragging you into a wild goose chase."

"Me, hate you too? Who else are you talking about?"

"Marie Thérèse. She insisted that I explain the real reasons for my being here, and she didn't like the answer at all. I've lost her friendship. She thought I was interested in looking for the fastest and most effective way to repatriate undocumented Haitians who are in the Dominican Republic, and maybe I want to do it because I'm racist."

"And did you not clarify? I find her reaction strange. Marie Thérèse doesn't strike me as being obtuse, I mean, some psycho who refuses to hear what anyone has to say."

"You're making me laugh with your observation! Yes, Marie Thérèse doesn't seem to be like that. With regard to your question about what I'm really looking for here, I want to see if this project that was supposed to benefit both Haiti and the Dominican Republic, which had been planned by the chancelleries of both countries and a bunch of international agencies for years, ever got implemented. But, everything seems to be easier said than done ..."

"Let's be optimistic, and hope you find what you're looking for," Marcel replied.

"If only everything were that simple. But this equation has a whole lot of variables, like political and hegemonic interests. It's the law of the funnel."

"That's true. There's no doubt about that."

"I have the impression that this project got mired in the bureaucracy of diplomacy and tangled up in the words of all its resolutions. And as if that were not enough, everybody's ego gets in the middle and must be included."

Gabriel pressed his lips together and turned his head away, feigning looking out the car window to disguise his frustration.

"What do you mean?"

"Lately many diplomats and high-ranking officials in these international organizations seem to pay more attention to their personal prestige, to whatever advancement they can get in their diplomatic careers, than to the public service they are duty-bound to provide to the nation they represent. Thank goodness there are still brilliant and excellent diplomats who still very much have their integrity."

"Their values have changed ... it's a shame. Well, dogs bite in every country. One has to hope that things will improve thanks to the actions of people like you, people with great hearts and noble souls. You're a good egg indeed, Gabriel."

"Marcel, you make me laugh. Thank you."

****

19

When Gabriel and Marcel arrived in Ouanaminthe, they met a crowd of over 3,000 Haitians who were waiting for the border to be opened. Marcel parked the Camry in one of the adjacent streets, and agreed with Gabriel to meet back at his car in two hours.

For Gabriel, crossing over to Dajabón felt like déjà vu. He felt the same nervousness and fear that had gripped him when he had mingled with the crowd on Market Day in Jimaní as the beginning of his adventure in Haiti just over a month ago.

His heart dropped when he arrived in Dajabón. Here, he found no trace of construction. He had hoped to find at least the skeleton of the structure of the Binational Market the Haitian and Dominican governments and international agencies had been planning for years. Hadn't they mentioned that the market would begin operating in September 2011? Unless somebody had a magic wand, the Binational Market wouldn't be built in three weeks as promised.

Gabriel allowed himself to drift in the sea of Dominican and Haitian traders like a leaf carried by a current. He recalled the devastation caused to that area at the beginning of the 17th century by Governor Antonio de Osorio under the orders of King Philip III of Spain to end the illegal trading the French, English, Dutch and even Portuguese were doing with the *hateros*, the cattlemen of the Spanish colony, to the detriment of the Spanish crown. Gabriel witnessed the commercial activity taking place in a chaotic stewpot of languages, overcrowding and unsanitary conditions, and just as in Jimaní, this activity was being carried out on a regular basis with the consent of authorities on both sides of the island. Why, then, it was it taking so long to implement a project for the same purpose that would benefit these communities, the two nations?

Obviously, large amounts of money were circulating there, not counting the cash being passed under the table, and the money from all the illegal transactions freely taking place under the mantle of corruption that covered both countries.

As Gabriel observed the situation, he recalled more Dominican history and some of the provisions of the Lomé IV Convention, especially the ones about human rights ... might that sword of Damocles hanging over the heads of the two countries, and the political instability reigning in Haiti all this time, be responsible for delaying the aid?

Gabriel shook off those thoughts. Perhaps the delay was due to the change of government in Haiti, which had a new president. It was just a matter of timing. He smiled. God's timing is perfect. Without realizing it, he had made it back to Marcel's car, where they had agreed to meet. Gabriel heard Marcel calling to him, waving with his arm to indicate where he was. Gabriel ran toward him.

"Marcel, let's get out of here as quickly as possible and look for a place to stay. This has been a crazy trip. I apologize for causing so much trouble. Honestly, I don't know why the hell you listened to me."

Marcel laughed as if he had heard the best joke in the world, and Gabriel, recognizing the pure absurdity and ridiculousness of the situation, exploded in laughter as well.

"Let's just say this is the first windmill we've faced, Don Quixote." Marcel's car was filled with laughter.

****

They arrived in Cap-Haïtien at 3:30 p.m., checking into a hotel after a meal of fried pork with fried plantains at a local restaurant. This was one of Marcel's favorite dishes.

"We're going to stay here tonight. I want to show you the attractions of this city. For the time being, forget about diplomacy and your research. Not everything is work, life is short and you have to live it," commented Marcel, as proud and satisfied as a peacock.

"Thank you for your generosity, and above all, thanks for being patient with me. Anyone else would have ripped my head off for what happened today. Instead, you're spoiling me."

"You are wrong, Gabriel. It isn't generosity, but gratitude. It's the least I can do to thank you and your people for the solidarity and cooperation we have received from you all ever since the earthquake."

Gabriel opened his mouth to answer, but no words came out. He stared into Marcel's eyes and saw that they were welling with tears. They hugged each other as if they were father and son, and then went quietly to their rooms to rest. They were dead tired.

****

20

Marie Thérèse had been working for two consecutive days at the center with Marianne. She had to struggle to keep her mind on what she was doing, because her mind continually strayed to the dialogue she wanted to have with Gabriel.

She dared not be the first to pick up the phone, first, because she didn't want to disturb him in case he really was attending to personal affairs, and second, because she knew this conversation wouldn't be appropriate for the phone. She kept thinking the worst, that they would never see each other again. A sort of restlessness fluttered like a moth between her stomach, head and heart. At last, she took some of the paper she had been using to make flyers, grabbed a pen, and sat down to write.

Friday, August 5, 2011

Dear Gabriel:

I don't dare call you. I want to believe you're out of town for personal reasons, like you told Antoine, and not because of what happened at the restaurant. I'm sorry about my reaction. I want you to know I'm not mad at you, or offended or insulted. What you said doesn't affect our friendship. You expressed yourself with the touch of the diplomat you are. I assure you, were I in your place, I would not have acted like this, but I would have been moved by my passion.

I regret I gave you the impression our friendship had to be bound by the straitjacket of nationalism and racism. Nothing could be further from the truth. In my opinion, at this point in the game of human history, those positions should not exist any more. We are all human beings, and that's what matters, or should.

My reaction at lunch had nothing to do with your position as a Dominican, nor as a jurist or as a trained diplomat, who was defending Dominican sovereignty according to the principles of national and international law. It rather had to do with my conscience being forced to wake up about the reality of my country, and, as you put it very well, of the island. I felt helpless in all respects, as a Haitian, a woman, and a professional. I saw myself reduced to nothing in front of the "external forces" that have dressed us up as Little Red Riding Hood ... the better to eat us. See, I'm getting stirred up again.

As I was saying, all of a sudden, I clearly saw that our situation was a big farce, and even though I work non-stop at the center and in rural communities trying to make a difference with what I do, the springtime I crave so much for my country will never come. And do you know why? This was the epiphany that left me speechless ... I realized that to achieve the future Haiti wants and deserves, all Haitians have to reach out and grab it together and forge it here and now, as when we first emerged as a nation. Isn't that how my ancestors did it?

Yes, Gabriel, we Haitians have to act now, moved by the same ideals of personal freedom, fraternity, and equality our ancestors fought for in order to reclaim our dignity as a people, as a nation, and at the same time, get out of the social, economic, and political quicksand we are submerged in now, a morass that we will seemingly not get out of, considering the conditions that have prevailed in my country since the earthquake.

That's why I was unable to speak when I heard what you were saying during lunch. My mouth was unable to say all the information my brain was sending to it.

I hope after you read this letter we can resume the conversation we never finished. I hope you have successfully resolved the issues that took you out of town.

See you soon,

Marie Thérèse Cadet.

Once she finished writing, Marie Thérèse grabbed an envelope from the drawer of the nightstand, slipped the letter into it, and wrote "Gabriel Novoa Ramírez" on the envelope. She would leave it at the reception desk of the Royal Inn early in the morning, in the hope that Gabriel would return that weekend and read it. With that idea in her mind, she turned off the light to go to sleep. She noticed that for the first time in almost 18 months, no images of the earthquake crept in to torture her; her mind was filled with pleasant images of a vehement Gabriel addressing the mothers in the field, of a firm Gabriel defending the rights of the Dominican Republic as a free state, sovereign and independent.

She awoke early and dressed up as if she were going out on a date. Indeed, deep down she was hoping she would run into Gabriel at the hotel so she could give him the letter personally. She felt quite self-assured until she reached the entrance of the Royal Inn. Then, a *frisson* of nervousness overtook her.

"Good morning," she greeted the receptionist in a barely audible voice,. "Could you inform me if Mr. Gabriel Novoa Ramírez is still booked here?"

"Please, give me a minute to verify the guest book. Yes, he's still booked here, but right now, he's out of town. Do you want to leave him a message?"

Marie Thérèse wordlessly opened her purse, took out the envelope, and handed it to her interlocutor.

"Please give this envelope to Mr. Novoa Ramírez as soon as he returns. Thanks a lot."

Marie Thérèse walked quickly out the door and away from the hotel, as if she were urgently needed somewhere else. In fact, she wanted to get away to calm down, because she'd felt as if her heart was trying to leap out of her chest since she had stopped by the reception desk. Her heart was beating so fast and vigorously that she was in pain and breathless.

****

21

On Saturday morning, after breakfast, Marcel and Gabriel ventured out to enjoy the cultural riches of Haiti's second largest city. They toured downtown Cap-Haïtien, where Marcel proudly showed off the famous gingerbread houses, the French colonial architecture, the main square, and the Cathedral of Cap-Haïtien.

"In general, people associate Haiti with voodoo. They completely ignore the fact that until 1987 Catholicism was the official religion and that 80% of the population is Catholic. Voodoo is the religion of the people, both religions coexist without any issues. There is also a minority group of Protestants. This cathedral dates back to 1670. The building suffered some damage from the earthquake of 1842, but as you can see, it's in beautiful condition thanks to the excellent renovation work done in 1941 and 1942. You'll see how pretty it is inside. The Place d'Armes, the square in front of it, is where the abolition of slavery was declared on August 29, 1793."

Gabriel gazed up at the two bell towers of the cathedral, one of which carried a clock; he also admired the statues of saints in niches and the capital-crowned columns of the façade. He was transported to Haiti's French colonial past and imagined the moment when Léger-Félicité Sonthonax and Étienne Polverel, the commissioners of the Legislative Assembly, proclaimed the abolition of slavery after they expelled, with the help of slaves, the English and Spanish forces fighting for the return of the French monarchy. Sonthonax and Polverel proclaimed the abolition of slavery to honor their agreement with the slaves to grant them freedom in exchange for their support in the struggle. Gabriel felt a lump in his throat just by imagining that historical event.

"Now I'll show you two monuments that were declared UNESCO World Heritage sites in 1982: The Laferrière Citadel and the Sans-Souci Palace. The Citadel is 27.3 kilometers south of the city, and the Sans-Souci Palace is about 5 kilometers from the Citadel."

When they dismounted from the Camry, Marcel's face was shining with pride and satisfaction.

"Look how impressive the Citadel is. It's the largest fortress in the Americas and the Western Hemisphere, with an area of about 10,000 square meters. It was built between 1805 and 1820 by 20,000 men on the orders of King Henri-Christophe to defend the new republic from French attacks. The workers used stones that they carried up the mountain themselves. To hold the stones together, they used a mortar mixture of lime, molasses, and cow's and goat's blood in the belief that the spirits and gods of the Voodoo religion would give power and strength to the structure."

Gabriel was visibly moved by the grandeur of the colossal Citadel, but above all, by the vehemence and pride with which Marcel presented the cultural treasures and history of his country. He imagined the determination of the workers for the first time, liberated slaves who were building a testimony to their struggle for equality and human dignity with each stone they put in place.

"Now I'll show you the Sans-Souci Palace, which was built 5 kilometers from the Citadel, in the town of Milot, because King Henri-Christophe wanted to minimize his vulnerability to attacks from the coast. The Sans-Souci Palace was built between 1810 and 1813 on the land of what had been the plantation of Milot during the Haitian Revolution, which Henri-Christophe himself had been managing during the Revolution. The ups and downs of life, eh? It was meant to be a replica of the Palace of Versailles, and is said to have been the most beautiful residence ever built in the Americas. In 1820, King Henri-Christophe committed suicide on the second floor, just above the suite of the palace where he slept, shooting himself with a silver bullet when he became incapacitated by a stroke and was no longer able to lead or command his troops. Unfortunately, the great earthquake of 1842, which almost devastated Cap-Haïtien, destroyed this architectural gem, but you can still see the main halls and terraces. The Chapel of Milot, where the king was crowned, can be seen from here, and that big Caimito tree you see there, near that statue, was the place where the king dispensed justice. The entire court would come down this walkway to stand before the Justice Tree, as it is known. It's three hundred years old."

Gabriel, transported by Marcel's evocative details, imagined the lavishness of the parties and the halls of the palace, Queen Marie-Louise and his two daughters, the court, and other prominent personalities of the time. Likewise, he imagined the soldiers in their barracks and the royal battery, or nobles strolling by the waterworks, through which water still flowed, bearing witness to the durability of the splendor that once shone there.

"Marcel, you don't know how much I appreciate this tour. I'm so moved by the history of your country and touched by your heartfelt descriptions of the sights you showed me in Cap-Haïtien. Now I understand why your face has been glowing with joy since early this morning."

"I just wanted you to see the riches of my land. Here in Haiti, we have so much to offer, and yet in the minds of so many people in the world, our country is equated with poverty and zombies. Of course, there is a lot of poverty, and even more now after the earthquake, but I think we can emerge from the ashes, if they would only let us be, if they would only give us the chance to rise up ..."

"I completely agree with you."

****

22

Gabriel took advantage of their growing closeness after the tour to encourage Marcel to continue their conversation, asking questions about his country's culture as they drove back to Port-au-Prince. Gabriel liked the fact that Marcel not only was a good listener, but a lively and learned interlocutor.

"I could swear you were a native of Cap-Haïtien from your enthusiasm when you talk about its cultural and historical treasures."

"You'd be right, Gabriel. I am. I was born and raised here. I studied at Our Lady of Perpetual Help School, a private boys' school. Then I moved to Port-au-Prince to study at the National University. Later, I worked there as a professor, until the day of the earthquake when we were all stripped of everything and our loved ones."

Marcel forcefully gripped the car's steering wheel and leaned forward, trying to concentrate on his driving. He clenched his jaw, feeling yet again the pain caused by the memories of that fateful day. His body language cried out his personal tragedy.

"I'm so sorry. At times like these, one can't find the words ..." Gabriel gently laid his hand on Marcel's shoulder.

"I know. Don't feel bad. I was the one who brought it up. And I did it because I feel like I'm talking to Victor, because I feel we have the same concerns. I have the conviction that genuine, goodhearted people like you will help and encourage my country to rise up."

"Like the phoenix."

"No, like the two-headed dragon, which according to Greek mythology arose from the blood that dripped from the Gorgon's head when Perseus cut it off and flew with it over the Libyan desert. This little dragon feeds on ants, and isn't dangerous despite the fact it breathes fire from its two mouths. It has the gift of survival and regeneration and the power to heal old wounds."

Gabriel kept thinking about how fitting the image and meaning of the two-headed dragon was for the circumstances of the island. Two heads, like the two nations, and the regeneration of their relationship. The nation of Haiti needed to cure the wounds of its past and those caused by the earthquake ... In fact, both nations had to heal their wounds in order for their relationship to be based on solidarity, cooperation, and action, instead of mistrust and reaction.

"I love that description, and your viewpoint. We now have to pray for political stability in Haiti to produce political, economic, and social development. Maybe that will get the Binational Market project moving in Dajabón, and other projects as well."

"May God hear you! Stability was supposedly guaranteed by the international community when it financed and managed the 2010 presidential election to impose its agenda. The people's will was not respected in the election; the international community made sure to eliminate, in the most grotesque way, in the name of "democracy and our institutions" the candidate who was favored by the Haitians and who defended our national interests."

Just as Gabriel was about to share his opinion on the 2010 Haitian presidential election, Marcel's Camry slowed to a stop in front of the Royal Inn. Gabriel once again was struck by the timing. Ever since his arrival in Haiti, he had been saved from compromising situations every single time he was about to walk into one.

"We're back; what an experience we've had," Marcel said, smiling broadly.

"Believe me, I can't say enough to thank you for your help and everything you've done for me. I'll be back at the center tomorrow. Get some rest, Marcel. And once again, thank you."

****

23

Gabriel entered the Royal Inn and went to the reception desk to reclaim the key to room 202, chatting briefly with the hotel receptionist, who welcomed him back, freely expressing his gratitude for each of his guests. The receptionist handed Gabriel the key along with the envelope Marie Thérèse had left for him. Gabriel looked at the envelope. It didn't have the sender's name on it, but he sensed it was a letter from Marie Thérèse.

"This morning, an elegant, beautiful young lady asked me to hand you that envelope as soon as I saw you come in," the receptionist mentioned with a mischievous smile.

"Thank you very much. I was waiting for her to drop it off," Gabriel said, feigning naturalness. "Good night."

Gabriel entered his room, laid the room key and envelope on the console where the TV was, and headed straight to the bathroom to take a shower and revitalize himself. He was dead tired from the long journey, and also wanted to quiet his mind. The developments Marcel had mentioned to him in his "nutshell summary" of the problems sinking the Haitian educational system were roiling about in his head.

When he came out of the bathroom, he grabbed the envelope, flipped on the bedside lamp, and climbed into bed with it. He opened it and began to read. After a few seconds, he sat up in bed, sliding some pillows behind his back to remain propped up. He read the letter once, twice. He checked the time on his watch and stared at the ceiling with the letter in his right hand. He pondered how to proceed, debating whether to call Marie Thérèse right then and there, or wait until morning to speak to her at the center. He dismissed this last option. Mustering his courage, he picked up his cell phone and dialed Marie Thérèse's number. She responded immediately, as if she were waiting for his call.

"Good evening, Marie Thérèse. It's Gabriel Novoa Ramirez."

"Gabriel, thank goodness you called me, thank goodness you're back. I thought we weren't going to hear from you anymore because of me. I imagine you read my letter."

"Yes, thank you for your explanation. You took a real weight off of my shoulders. Honestly, I was worried about your reaction."

"No need to worry, Gabriel. There's no reason to stay away from the center. I'm not angry or offended."

"I'm relieved about that, Marie Thérèse," said Gabriel. "Actually, I did have some personal affairs to straighten out. After what I learned today, I have to see how best to keep my word to Antoine to help him at the center and how best to do what I need to do with respect to other things."

"What do you mean?"

"I'd better explain it to you tomorrow in person. Good night, Marie Thérèse."

"Until tomorrow, Gabriel. You get some rest now. Good night."

Ensconced in her bed, Marie Thérèse curled up with her phone in her hand, wondering what Gabriel learned that had changed the course of his actions in Haiti, and in her wondering, she fell asleep.

Gabriel kept thinking about his conversation with Marcel during their trip back to Port-au-Prince, and the more he analyzed what they had discussed, the more he wondered who Marcel Vincent really was. When Victor told him he would find him a host, it never crossed his mind that it would be someone like Marcel, so knowledgeable, learned, and passionate about his country.

Instinctively, he picked up his phone again and searched the Internet and social media. A photo of Marcel popped up on the screen with some text below it, confirming what he was looking for. Gabriel read the brief paragraph under the photo: "One of the great intellectuals of Haitian society, professor of philosophy and sociology at the School of Humanities of the National University."

With this discovery, Gabriel felt the pieces of the puzzle of his life fall into place for the first time since he'd embarked on this adventure in Haiti. And with the joy of his discovery, he switched off the bedside lamp to go to sleep, uttering praise to God in his mind and heart:

God, thank you, thank you for holding me in the palm of Your hand ... Now more than ever I know you are guiding me. Thank you, Lord, thank you!

****

24

Gabriel woke up earlier than usual, wanting to talk to Marcel as soon as possible. He had so many questions to ask him, and he also had to honor his commitment to Antoine and Marie Thérèse. However, Gabriel sensed that the course of his life would depend on his next conversation with Marcel.

"Good morning, Marcel. It's Gabriel Novoa Ramírez."

"Good morning, Gabriel, I recognized your voice. Is everything okay?"

"Sorry to call you so early. It's that I was thinking about what we talked about yesterday ... Well, now that I know who you are, I really feel that I need your help; I feel that it's through you that I'm going to find what I'm looking for."

Marcel paused for a second, then responded. "Can we get together at 3:00 p.m.? I have another commitment earlier in the day that I can't change."

"Excellent! Where do you want us to meet?"

"I can pick you up at the center. You mentioned you'd be working there again, right?"

"Yes. I'll see you at 3:00 p.m. at the center. Thank you, Marcel. Thank you."

Gabriel headed to the hotel restaurant and had scrambled eggs with toast and black coffee for breakfast. As soon as he finished, he left the hotel in a hurry to meet Antoine and the other volunteers at the center.

When Gabriel arrived, he found Antoine dealing with a thousand details for this place where 200 children were sheltered, ranging in age between 7 and 17 years old. Of this group of 200 children, 150 were girls.

"Gabriel, good to see you! It's as if you've dropped down from Heaven! " Antoine exclaimed as soon as he looked up and saw him. "There are two volunteers who aren't coming in today ..."

"Don't worry, Antoine, just tell me what I have to do." Gabriel followed Antoine to the back of the center.

Marie Thérèse arrived at nine o'clock in the morning and began organizing the activities she would be carrying out with the other volunteers that day. She caught sight of Gabriel helping the psychological support staff document reports of abuse from two children who had shown up at the center. Marie Thérèse greeted him warmly.

"See, Gabriel, this ship sails where the wind blows."

"Yes, Antoine has explained to me that at the center, things change constantly, and we have to improvise and go with the flow, take things as they come."

Marie Thérèse nodded and went to the first classroom to continue teaching the children how to write their name and how to read and write.

When she finished the tasks of the day, she left the center and stood by the door, waiting to meet Gabriel as soon as he walked out. She was excited as a schoolgirl waiting to see her crush. She kept looking towards the door, hoping to see him step out at any moment. But it was Marcel Vincent she saw on the street, getting out of his car. Her heart sank. She knew her plans to be with Gabriel that evening had come to naught, and felt frustrated.

"I imagine you're coming for Gabriel. Good afternoon, Marcel," said Marie Thérèse, a little annoyed at how frustrated she felt.

"Good afternoon, Marie Thérèse. Yes, we agreed to meet here."

"Gabriel told me he was going to speak with you, but I didn't think he would do it here." Curiosity consumed her.

Marcel remained silent. He noted the body language of Marie Thérèse, who despite her effort to pretend cordiality, was tense and annoyed. Marcel thought it best to go into the center and get Gabriel, but at that very moment Gabriel came out the door, and walked over to where Marcel and Marie Thérèse were standing.

"I apologize for the delay, Marcel, but it took me longer than I thought to finish what Antoine needed me to do. Marie Thérèse, well, to paraphrase what you said this morning, we have to sail where the wind blows. We'll have to adjust the sails … we'll talk soon."

Gabriel lightly touched Marie Thérèse's right shoulder, and without giving her time to answer, he walked with Marcel to where the Camry was parked.

****

25

Gabriel started talking as soon as he got into the car. He was filled with hope and excitement over what he had discovered the night before. He felt as joyful as a child on Christmas morning.

"Marcel, last night I learned who you really are. When Victor told me he would contact a friend of his to help me while I was in Haiti, I thought maybe it would be a relative, never an intellectual so important to Haitian society. Ever since I arrived, you've dedicated yourself to providing me with the information I need. It wasn't until yesterday that I connected all the dots, when you mentioned your time as a professor at the National University and your personal experiences, and I saw your profile on social media."

"And what surprises you the most? To find out who I am, or to find out what I'm doing now for a living?"

"Both, and neither. I see the hand of God in all this so clearly. I do not believe in coincidence, but in divine incidence. And this is one of them. It really surprised me, this connection I've felt with you since we met. At first, I thought you felt sorry for me, that you were helping me because you thought I'd fallen apart when I realized that people had forgotten Haiti's devastation, which is as unchanged as if it had just happened. Then, I thought maybe you owed Victor a favor and you were paying him back by helping me. But then, yesterday I finally saw the spiritual and intellectual connection between us, when you talked about the Haitian educational system and the two-headed dragon."

"Interesting. Well, Gabriel, it's been a two-way street. When Victor asked me to help you, I thought you'd be just one more of these countless press correspondents who have come to Haiti to narrate our misery. I knew your adventure in search of knowledge and solutions to the island's challenges was like the quest I myself embarked on in January 2010, when the earthquake destroyed my professional and personal world. When I saw your genuine interest in fellowship and solidarity, I knew that you are the kind of person both countries need in order to get us out of the hole we're in."

Gabriel realized Marcel had driven well past the Royal Inn and was now driving into an area he wasn't familiar with.

"Where are we going? I thought we were going to talk at the restaurant at the Royal Inn."

"We'll have dinner later. First, I want you to meet a group of people I know will interest you and can help you in your research of Haiti's reality."

Marcel laughed when he saw Gabriel's puzzled face, trying to figure out the mystery.

"Nothing illegal, of course!" Marcel roared with laughter, and Gabriel couldn't help but join in.

"Marcel, that idea *never* crossed my mind."

They arrived at a house with obvious repairs to reinforce the structure. Marcel parked his Camry in the street and together they walked toward the house. There, Gabriel met four people who he later discovered were Marcel's colleagues.

"Gentlemen, I present to you Gabriel Novoa Ramírez, a Dominican brother, who is in our country studying our current reality. Gabriel, these are my chosen brothers, who are united by the ideal of a free, quality public education for all Haitians. Under the banner of our cause and our efforts, we are providing the Haitian government with the tools and concepts for restructuring the Haitian educational system. It is our moral and citizen duty to save Haiti's Democratic destiny."

Gabriel talked for an hour and a half with these scholars and intellectuals, sharing his viewpoints on the importance of mandatory public education in Haiti, and the need to end the institutionalization of private education, which was interested only in the advantages to be gained from international subsidies that were supposed to be given to Haiti but only ended up benefiting vested interests to the detriment of the Haitian people.

After the meeting and during dinner, Marcel and Gabriel spoke of other related topics, during which Marcel, as a sociologist and connoisseur of Haitian history, seized the occasion to point out why the state of Haiti had failed.

"People must learn the lessons taught by history in order to not make the same mistakes," Marcel commented when he parked his car in front of the Royal Inn. "Tomorrow I'll introduce you to another group of people who I think will help you manifest your purpose. Good night, my friend. Get some rest."

"Good night, Marcel. Thanks for everything. I'm so honored," Gabriel responded, looking into his host's eyes. He got out of the car and walked into the Royal Inn with a lightness in his heart.

****

When Gabriel entered his room he had the urge to call Marie Thérèse immediately. He looked at the clock and thought she might be having dinner. He decided to wait. He spent that time thinking about the people he had met that day and what Marcel had taught him. After he showered, he got into bed and waited another fifteen minutes to dial Marie Thérèse.

"Good evening, Marie Thérèse, I hope I'm not disturbing you," said Gabriel when she answered the phone.

"Not at all. I was waiting for your call. How did it go with Marcel?"

"Great! You have no idea how grateful I am to God for putting Marcel in my path.

He is without a doubt the person I needed to connect with in order to fulfill my purpose. And I think he could help you, too."

"Umm ... what do you mean?"

"I'm talking about everything you said in the letter you wrote to me and your wish for Haiti to rise from the ashes. If you will allow me, I can show Marcel your letter; I'm sure he can guide you, like he's doing for me. Do you know who Marcel is?"

"No, I guess he's a good friend of Antoine? I've seen them conversing many times at the center."

"They may be good friends, but Marcel is also one of Haiti's intellectual giants, and he is fighting for the revival of this country along with other people who feel and think like he does."

"And you do not see that as a threat to the sovereignty of your country?"

"Not at all. We have reached a point in the history of our two nations where mistrust and past resentments must be left behind. As I told you, I believe Haiti and the Dominican Republic can and must coexist in a framework of harmony, brotherhood, solidarity, and respect for one another's sovereignty. Every time I talk to Marcel, I become more convinced of this diplomatic position, which obviously must be based on political, economic, and social relationships with the same ideals. I am convinced the economic self-sufficiency of the island must be the basis for these relationships to flourish and strengthen."

"You're right, Gabriel, it's our only way out. Please, by all means show my letter to Marcel; I would like to know his take on it, and if I can be part of his team."

"Of course! I am firmly convinced that we will be united for a great cause. Well, now I'm going to let you rest. I'll see you tomorrow."

"Until tomorrow, Gabriel. And thank you for calling me. Good night."

****

26

Marie Thérèse awoke with a start in the middle of the night, filled with fear and confusion. She switched on the bedside lamp, squinting at the light. She was drenched in sweat and felt the room spinning around her. She leaned slowly back against the mattress and breathed deeply in an attempt to quell her dizziness. As she lay in bed, she asked the spirits if the symptoms she was experiencing were due to a bad dream, not the virus that had affected two of her coworkers who had fallen ill with stomach distress. She prayed the discomfort was something transient, not cholera. Since the epidemic had erupted in Haiti, she was terrified of the idea of contracting it. After a few minutes, she sat up and went to the bathroom to look for medications in the medicine cabinet. She convinced herself that all was well, so she only drank some water with baking soda and fell asleep.

Marie Thérèse woke up again, and this time she was unable to go back to sleep. She had learned to cope with her insomnia by using this time for creative pursuits like drawing, or journaling about her experiences in Haiti.

She thought of Gabriel and the projects being spearheaded by Marcel and his collaborators, and sighed. She grabbed some of the paper she used to make flyers for the center's campaign against child abuse. She was going to work on that, but instead the image of Marcel came to her mind, and she wrote him.

Dear Marcel:

Gabriel has spoken very enthusiastically about the projects you are carrying out to rebuild Haiti through education. I recognize that this is remarkable work. However, the magnitude of the challenges we have in our country leads me to wonder whether your efforts will bear fruit, given the seriousness of the conditions under which this country is suffering. I apologize for my audacity and ignorance; I know how highly qualified and knowledgeable about Haitian society you are, but I do not understand how this awakening of our collective consciousness will take place when we lack everything, and from the viewpoint of a person down in the trenches like me, I think certain things are necessary in order for people to be receptive, and above all, provide the fertile soil where the seeds you are planting could germinate. I am referring to infrastructure, buildings for housing schools, a good transportation network in order to have access to them, and basic services such as drinking water, sanitation, and electrical power; to governmental and institutional restructuring in order to effectively implement policies and provisions; to an economic restructuring that would allow our economy to grow, activate our agriculture, promote industrial development, and generate jobs to improve Haiti's quality of life.

I want to be optimistic, I want to see the Haiti you envision ... but, after seeing so many promises being broken and hearing so many times about so many projects that would give splendor to Haiti, which unfortunately, remain just ideas, I think my mind and my heart have been hardened, because again, I do not see how Haiti will rise from the ashes.

I'm going to ask Gabriel to deliver this letter. I also told him it was okay to show you the letter I wrote to him. I want to be part of your team; I want to be part of your dream.

I have dared to put my ideas in writing only for now, because I do not know if I'll be able to discuss these issues with you in person without offending you or getting emotional. Please forgive my forthrightness, but I wanted you to understand my viewpoint and my concerns.

Sincerely,

Marie Thérèse Cadet.

Marie Thérèse folded the letter and slid it into an envelope which she addressed to Marcel Vincent. Then she picked up another sheet of paper and began to design the next batch of flyers to hand out to rural mothers about the plight of the restaveks.

****

27

Marie Thérèse showed up at the center the next day as usual and worked with the enthusiasm of knowing the positive impact her efforts were having on the lives of the young people she served. Gabriel worked alongside her just as enthusiastically. The camaraderie that existed between them, and especially the devotion with which they carried out their tasks, filled their workspace with good cheer.

As evening approached, they left the center as lighthearted as a teenaged couple going for a walk in the park.

"Why don't we have dinner together to talk about Marcel's projects?"

"That would be nice! Do you want to go to the restaurant at the Royal Inn's restaurant? I think it would be the perfect setting for mending fences." Marie Thérèse folded her arms and looked askance at Gabriel with a flirtatious grin, referring to her behavior the last time they had dined there.

"Oh, please, say no more," said Gabriel, feigning seriousness before a burst of mischievous laughter betrayed him. Marie Thérèse heartily returned the laughter.

When they arrived at the Royal Inn, they headed straight over to the restaurant and sat at the same table in the back corner.

"I wrote to Marcel last night," Marie Thérèse remarked in a rush as if she were in a race with the server, who was already heading to the table with a basket of rolls.

"Interesting! I have the letter you wrote me. I was going to call Marcel and see if he could come have dinner with us and formally introduce you two."

"Perfect! Yes, please, call him. I really want to talk to him, hear his opinion about my doubts and concerns."

Gabriel took out his cell phone and promptly called Marcel with the dinner invitation. Twenty minutes later, Marcel arrived and joined Marie Thérèse and Gabriel at the table.

"I think you may have noticed that I am a creature of habit," Gabriel told Marcel with a broad smile. "I'm starting to feel like the Royal Inn is my second home."

"I'm glad to hear that!" replied Marcel with a nod and smile to Marie Thérèse.

"I know you already know each other casually and that you've spoken briefly on other occasions, but I want to take this opportunity to introduce the two of you formally. Marie Thérèse, this is Marcel Vincent, professor of the School of Humanities at the National University, and Marcel, this is Marie Thérèse Cadet, a publicist who was living in Montreal, Canada when the earthquake hit, and has been here in Port-au-Prince since January 2010."

Marcel and Marie Thérèse both chuckled at Gabriel's charming introduction protocol. The server came up to add a service for three to the table and ask if they were ready to order. They ordered the fried pork with fried plantains that Marcel enjoyed so much. Gabriel took the letter Marie Thérèse had written to him from his shirt pocket.

"I want to share this with you." Gabriel handed the envelope to Marcel, who took it with a look of mild surprise. Marcel began to read the letter. As soon as he finished, Marcel gazed into Marie Thérèse's eyes as intensely as if he were scanning her soul. He was about to tell her something, but Marie Thérèse didn't give him time to speak.

"I wrote you a letter, too, Marcel; it may come across as insolent, but it is not. I don't mean to offend you, but to understand you." She handed her own envelope to Marcel.

Marcel set out to read the letter Marie Thérèse had written him. He laid it down on the table in silence Marie Thérèse's face reflected anguish, while Gabriel's reflected curiosity.

"You can let Gabriel read it," said Marie Thérèse in a thread of a voice.

Marcel passed it to Gabriel, who read it eagerly. He felt Marcel and Marie Thérèse's eyes fixed on him, as if they were awaiting his verdict.

"I have the impression we're going to need a full seven-course dinner so that we'll have enough time to address all these issues," Gabriel commented with a twinkle in his eye. "What do you think?"

They all nodded while laughing.

"Brilliant, Marie Thérèse. Your remarks are very thoughtful and valid. Everything you mention in your letter is necessary for materializing Haiti's reconstruction. Your question is, how will that happen?"

The server came back just as Marcel was about to go further. They moved ahead with ordering the entire dinner at once, so that the server would only need to approach the table to pick up and bring out dishes without interrupting the flow of their conversation. As soon as the server left, Marcel turned to Marie Thérèse and Gabriel.

"Haiti's reconstruction ..." Marcel began, settling in his chair as if he were sitting at his desk in front of his classroom at the National University, "will occur with the active participation of Haitian citizens and those who are directly involved with implementing reconstruction projects. I mean to say, when individuals in the administration, the elite minorities of Haitian society, and even the Haitian diaspora all take action by assuming a leadership of authenticity and integrity that will make us better individuals, and thus, a better nation."

"All of that sounds great, but how would it be achieved in practice, really? Under the conditions we're in, we would have to start from scratch," Marie Thérèse interrupted.

"I was getting there. It will be achieved with an awakening of Haiti's consciousness, individually and collectively. An awakening that sets us on a path to a new way of being and doing things based on the commitment and participation of Haitian citizens in promoting and guaranteeing order, freedom, justice, respect, solidarity, honesty, and transparency. As you can guess, this can only be achieved through education and the instruction that political and social institutions should encourage, starting with the family, then the schools and other institutions. To create a new Haiti, we have to cultivate a new mindset, a new culture. I say Haiti, because it is our reality, but the template would really fit any country. This template would also put an end to many of the social ills that are affecting different countries. That's another advantage."

"Under the current conditions, with all the outside interference, I mean, with U.S. troops and blue helmets in the country and the implementation of agendas that do not necessarily benefit Haitians, how do you think the elite minorities of Haitian society will suddenly seek the common good?" Gabriel wondered while cutting into a piece of the roast chicken he'd ordered.

"Let me give you an example. Suppose that Marie Thérèse gets in touch with some company she knows in Montreal, let's say a company of engineers who wants to invest here, then, they seek out a Haitian counterpart, and a stretch of road is built to link two important regions in the country. Was my explanation clear? The actions of ordinary people will serve as the bricks for the foundation of a new nation."

"Um, excuse me, Marcel, not to play the devil's advocate, but how can one build housing for everyone who's been displaced by the earthquake or participate in infrastructure projects if international agencies and government institutions are supposed to be the ones to carry those out?" asked Marie Thérèse.

"Well, with Haitian entrepreneurs, as I mentioned; with the active participation of Haitians like you and me. That's why I'm so involved in this process. I invite you to come with us to see what we're doing so you'll understand it's not so different from what you're doing to help Haitian children."

Gabriel was intrigued by their observations about the elite minorities of Haiti. How could 1% of the population control 50% of Haiti's economy?

"Marcel, could you roughly give me, or rather, give us, an explanation of how the minorities in Haiti became so powerful?"

"With pleasure. It goes back to when we declared our independence. When the Haitian Republic emerged, the community of nations back then isolated it because Haiti's independence was considered as a threat to the colonialist economic model. In addition to the isolation imposed by other countries, Haiti had a self-imposed isolation as well. I'll explain. Haiti banned all foreign investments for fear that it might reintroduce slavery; foreigners could not own land. For 13 years after we declared our independence, Haitian society was deprived of durable institutions and the government was overwhelmed by the debt France had imposed in exchange for recognizing Haiti's independence and the high cost of maintaining a standing army, whose members ascended socially and formed a new minority. Aside from this group, there was a very small group of 'lightskins': English, French, Germans, some Americans who controlled exports and imports in the port cities; they gained power because they knew about Haiti's riches and succeeded in benefiting from them, in an environment of political instability. Besides these people, we also had the bureaucratic class, professionals serving the state. In other words, the military, large landowners, and traders had political and economic control of Haiti. A new variable was added to this equation: an influx of Syrian Christian immigrants at the end of the nineteenth century. Haiti wanted to stop this immigration and decided to go so far as to put it in our Constitution. The Haitian Constitution of 1897 stipulated that migrants who were not authorized by commercial treaties to settle in Haiti had to sign an agreement that they would live in the countryside and devote themselves to agriculture independently or under private landowners. However, this provision was rendered useless when France and the U.S. granted citizenship to the Syrians so that they were now able to purchase land and control our trade. At that time, foreign trade was controlled by foreign traders and only one of our nine coffee exporters was Haitian. Haitian involvement was greater in rum and liquor exports. By 1890, 70% of foreign trade was in international hands. France was the destination of 75% of our exports, and 70% of our imports came from the United States. Here comes the answer to your question, Gabriel: foreign traders held economic power, and through the ambassadors of their respective countries of origin, they interfered in domestic affairs by financing different groups in conflict and even interfered with the government itself, disrupting Haiti's financial equilibrium. The pattern has not changed, and the reason why is that in societies deprived of their institutions like Haitian society, crises are resolved and society is controlled by brute force."

Marcel drank a bit of water and gazed into Gabriel and Marie Thérèse's eyes, gauging their reaction, waiting for them to ask more questions or offer more comments.

"Thank you for the explanation. I love how you are able to summarize such complex historical, political, economic, and social issues in simple words and concepts in your famous 'nutshell summaries.' You're a true master."

"I agree with Gabriel. I think it's great too."

Marcel, Gabriel, and Marie Thérèse continued discussing Haiti and how to achieve its reconstruction long after they had finished eating.

"We must meet up again. It's a shame I have to go," Marcel apologized, looking at his watch and rising from his seat.

"I agree with you, Marcel. We've had quite an enriching discussion, and a pleasant evening." Gabriel stood up beside Marcel.

"Marie Thérèse, let me take you back to your hotel." Marcel offered.

"Accepted with pleasure, but Marcel, I must warn you that you'll be exposing yourself to the torture of my endless questions."

"I'm not afraid, I like a good challenge," Marcel replied, laughing and gently pulling out Marie Thérèse's chair so their beautiful companion could stand up.

****

28

Once Marie Thérèse made it to her room, she threw herself into bed. She was exhausted. The day had been long, and she knew she needed some sound rest. She grabbed one of the pillows and hugged it close to soften the loneliness. She knew the night would be a long one due to the insomnia that beset her relentlessly. However, tonight, instead of images of the rescue efforts after the earthquake or of her compatriots falling ill with cholera, her mind was replaying images of the dinner with Marcel and Gabriel at the Royal Inn. She saw the great emotional affinity between the two men, as if they were father and son. At an intellectual level, she saw them as two fishes happily swimming in a sea of knowledge, mutual admiration, and respect; they expressed their viewpoints freely and honestly, no matter how thorny they were. She, on the other hand, saw herself as a fish out of the water in which Marcel and Gabriel swam.

I feel so stagnant ... or really, more like I'm trapped with my country in going backwards into annihilation. I feel like Haiti is disappearing with each passing day; It's becoming invisible, and so am I along with it. The spirits know how much I want to believe in everything Marcel said at dinner ... I need to believe him, so I can get out of this black hole I'm in.

Umm ... Maybe the spirits sent me a sign with Marcel's model for Haiti's rebirth. What if that's exactly what I'm supposed to do? It makes sense, but by logic alone, how can you encourage investment in Haiti when there's no country to invest in? The first thing they'll point out is the lack of transparency for awarding projects, the corruption in our political and social institutions, the absence of a legal framework to define and guarantee the enforcement of new laws and societal stability.

Perhaps If I look at my country from a bird's eye view, flying far above the fray, I can figure out an advertising campaign to promote the direct foreign investment that Marcel was urging. If I start to think about all the challenges we face, it'll make me want to throw in the towel. To act, we must look for an axis, a supporting frame of reference. Enough of so many ideas and projects dying for lack of action. It occurs to me the change we are longing for will come out of our vulnerability. It is the law of life, the very cycle of nature, where what is built, is destroyed, then built again...

Marie Thérèse put the pillow aside, got up from the bed, opened the nightstand drawer and pulled out a notepad and pen. She was determined to design an advertising campaign to attract economic investment based on Marcel's observations. She closed her eyes, concentrated, and let her ideas flow to develop marketing and advertising strategies for foreign investment in Haiti.

Haiti, A Blank Slate was the first idea she wrote in big letters .Then, the names of various people flowed quickly from her pen in a burst of writing. She put her pen aside and read what she had written, and had a sort of an epiphany.

Ah! Marcel's right. It is the social commitment of Haitians that will bring about a cultural and economic change, and thus the rise of Haiti. The involvement of the Haitian diaspora will play a key role in the reconstruction of the country, in the promotion of private investment.

Excited, Marie Thérèse laid her notebook and pen on top of the nightstand and flipped off the light. If only dawn would come soon so she could share her ideas with Marcel and Gabriel. She wanted to show Marcel her commitment, her ideas, and her capabilities ... and as for Gabriel, she wanted to show him they shared the same ideals and aspirations.

****

29

Gabriel entered his room and began to reflect on the conversation at dinner with Marcel and Marie Thérèse. He paced around the little hotel room pondering Marcel's views, which transported him to his time as a student of diplomacy and international law.

Marcel's ideas reminded him in particular of a thesis he'd written about the possibility of an economic confederation between Haiti and the Dominican Republic as a platform for the entry of both countries into the Lomé Convention. He imagined himself back in college, standing behind the podium speaking to his geopolitics class about his thesis. Don Emilio was seated in the front row with two other professors he'd invited for the occasion.

Oh my God! It's been so long since that day, and yet it feels like yesterday. It is incredible that everything I wrote back then is still valid, especially considering the current circumstances of the island, with a Haiti in dire straits and a Dominican Republic totally overwhelmed by the weight of the situation. The only thing that's changed is the relationship the two countries ... before the earthquake, it was ruled by suspicion and mistrust, now there's solidarity. Yes, the earthquake has shaken the very foundation of this relationship to make evident the need for understanding in order to have sustainable mutual economic development on the island.

What we need to do now is to implement signed agreements under a coherent and institutionalized foreign policy through the Binational Joint Commission. Of course, the Dominican Republic's biggest challenge is that it will have to adapt its relations with Haiti to United States hegemony and that country's plans for Haiti.

Gabriel continued to recollect and ponder the impact of the informal commercial interactions between Haiti and the Dominican Republic across five border provinces and fourteen border towns; exchanges turned Haiti into the Dominican Republic's second largest trade partner after the earthquake. Gabriel went to the bathroom and showered. When he came out, he sat on the edge of the bed like an automaton. His mind was fixed on all the steps that would facilitate and implement a common market on the border that could make the island self-sufficient, if production were increased on both sides, especially in Haiti, where increased productivity would bring social stability to Haiti, which could in turn reduce the flow of migrants to the Dominican Republic.

It is a matter of formalizing the activities of buyers and sellers by creating physical and administrative infrastructures for carrying out these activities, the establishment of common policies through a customs union, preferential tariffs for products coming from Haiti, and a uniform payment system that facilitates commercial and financial exchange. And also, establishing the necessary controls to prevent illegal activities that could occur under the umbrella of the commercial interactions and threaten the safety of the island's inhabitants.

Of course, for this story to have a happy ending, we must end the apathy of governments, their lack of respect for the law and the agreements they've signed. This would be the first obstacle to overcome in order to make this common market a reality. How has this situation not changed despite the two governments signing an agreement in 1996 under the Binational Joint Commission? The second obstacle is the low profile the Dominican Republic is forced to maintain in its relations with Haiti, especially with regard to the economic development both countries need. The actions of the Dominican government must not go against the hegemonic agenda of the United States and the other countries with interests in Haiti, to prevent them from clipping the island's wings.

Gabriel dropped into bed, physically and mentally exhausted.

****

30

The next day, after Marie Thérèse and Gabriel worked with the *restaveks*, they got in touch with Marcel to see when they could meet up with him to discuss the ideas they had come up with after dinner. Marie Thérèse also wanted to meet the people involved with Marcel in his national reconstruction project. But Marcel already had a previous commitment, so they all agreed to get together when the next meeting of collaborators would be held.

"I feel like I'll be joining a secret society," Marie Thérèse joked, thinking about the upcoming meeting with Marcel.

"In a sense it is, because the participants are assuming a commitment to a noble and common ideal, but I promise you there is nothing secret about it; on the contrary, Marcel wants more people to participate in his efforts to bring about free public education for all Haitians."

"You mean Marcel is carrying out an indoctrination campaign at these meetings."

"Not at all," replied Gabriel. "Marcel is carrying out a philanthropic campaign. He seeks to eliminate the scourge of illiteracy and ignorance with each school that will be built with the help of those participating in their construction."

"If you don't mind, let's keep talking about this where I'm staying," invited Marie Thérèse, "so I can share the ideas that popped into my head last night for helping Marcel."

"I'd be delighted. I was up late too, brainstorming about what we'd discussed. I was looking for a way to expand the economic activity occurring at the border."

Gabriel and Marie Thérèse spent the remainder of the afternoon discussing how to work with Marcel, and the campaign for the *restaveks* as well.

****

After dinner, Marcel contacted Marie Thérèse to tell her the time and date of the next meeting with his collaborators. It would take place at the house he had taken Gabriel to. On this occasion, Paul, a good friend of Marcel's would be speaking on the importance of microenterprise.

"Marie Thérèse, I hope you can come. I think you'll like what you're going to hear and learn about; we're not only interested in promoting free public education in order to bring about change, but also in vocational training to facilitate access to credit for microenterprise," Marcel commented on the phone.

"You can count on me, Marcel. I'll get in touch with Gabriel and let him know so we'll come together. Thanks for the invitation," answered Marie Thérèse, filled with anticipation.

There were around 15 people in the house that served as the headquarters for Marcel's meetings, all listening thoughtfully to the details offered by a tall, slender man with the dignified bearing of a longtime government official. Gabriel and Marie Thérèse drew closer to the group to hear what he was saying.

"This type of training will especially help women in the poorest and most vulnerable areas of our country. They would be able to achieve a level of productivity that could help support one or more families while they become fully integrated into the economic process," explained Paul Boyer. "For example, they can be trained to raise chickens and produce eggs, making small-scale production and trade cooperatives that could then grow much larger, where they could produce artisan goods become skilled workers, tailors, or even builders."

"It's great to see the passion with which they're developing these cooperative projects to empower people and turn the people studying and working in these projects into business owners and employers," Marie Thérèse whispered to Gabriel.

Marcel, seated behind them, overheard her comment and leaned forward to add his thoughts to it. "Yes, Marie Thérèse, we want to expand this model outside of Port-au-Prince by searching for regional markets where we can create new workplaces. Imagine, half of our women engage in economic activity outside the home, and they represent 52% of the population. We are creating community councils and bringing together partners to get this sector of society, which is Haiti's civil society, inserted into the production process."

They spent the rest of the afternoon engaged in conversations with Marcel's colleagues, who crowded around Paul Boyer to ask questions and learn more details about the people involved in launching the initiative and the sectors where it would take place.

****

31

As Marie Thérèse and Gabriel got involved in the activities being organized by Marcel Vincent to restructure the Haitian educational system and promote the participation of private initiatives in the marginalized sectors of Haiti's economy , in the Dominican Republic the immigration situation became more controversial and worrisome due to the overwhelming presence of Haitians, which increased the Dominicans' fears and the conviction that a passive invasion was seemingly being carried out with the consent of Dominican authorities under the mantle of "solidarity." Haitians were displacing Dominicans in all sectors of Dominican society.

"Give 'em an inch and they'll take a mile," Amarilis Pantaleon argued in front of the Nuestra Señora de La Altagracia maternity ward, along with other Dominican women who were being forced to wait for Haitian women in labor to give birth first in order to receive care and give birth themselves.

"This is an abuse!" exclaimed Carmela Rondón, another Dominican woman in labor, to a doctor hurrying past the irate crowd into the building. "Haitian women are being bused in from Haiti as if they were tourists to give birth here. Explain that to me! This is outrageous! This country is screwed!"

The national press echoed the big question on Dominican citizens' minds: how was it possible that the Ministry of Public Health had spent 3 billion pesos on hospital services of pregnant Haitians and their children?

And despite the binational agreements and treaties signed by the two countries to prevent the trafficking of immigrants, minors, women and false documents, these activities were still occurring daily, becoming a very lucrative businesses for the parties involved.

What are Dominican government, immigration, law enforcement and judiciary officials doing about this? was another question on the lips of the press, who were denouncing the steep prices being demanded for falsified birth certificates and identity cards.

In response to such questions and to silence the population's outcry, the Dominican president gathered his cabinet to announce Decree 631-11 of October 19, 2011 on the execution of General Law 285-04 on Migration.

"Your excellency, this heated immigration situation," said the foreign affairs minister, "must be handled by your government with kid gloves to avoid more accusations of human rights violations from cropping up."

"I understand your viewpoint, and for that reason we are gathered in a special session," replied the Dominican president. "I want total transparency in the implementation of our immigration provisions so these international organizations won't come back to bite us on that matter."

"We have roughly estimated there are almost 400,000 undocumented Haitians in our country; we cannot waste more time with ineffective remedies, especially when many of the immigrants coming here feel they are above the law, disrespecting and provoking law enforcement authorities," disagreed the minister of the interior and national police.

"We've been generous to the Haitian government and nation and shown our solidarity with them and then some, but we can no longer carry the burden they pose to our government and our resources. At first, we thought the massive influx of Haitians was temporary; that most of those who fled here would go back to Haiti once the reconstruction process would begin with all the international aid that was coming in. At this point, we all know that has not come to pass, so we must act as soon as possible."

Before concluding the meeting, the President looked at each of his ministers with a serious expression. The ministers of education, public health, labor, agriculture, and tourism, as well as the attorney general, wore grim expressions as well, intensely aware of the impending storm they had yet to face.

****

The Dominican population seemed to be reassured by the new measures and actions the executive branch decreed to control immigration. The national press chronicled that sentiment, as well as the growing suspicion of some political commentators who saw in these measures a political gambit in view of the national elections coming up in 2012. Would this decree to quell irregular mass migration be stymied by the same inertia as the General Law on Migration? they wondered, and rightly so.

"Learn from other people's mistakes, Pierre. With one leg shorter than the other, you can't run any more. You can't run away to keep them from sending you back to Haiti."

Pierre Selvandieu repeated this mantra in his mind as he tended the little shop where worked selling used clothes in Petit-Haiti, the Haitian quarter located behind Modelo Market on Avenida Mella; little enclave in the capital where Haitians sold all kinds of goods and even broken items, in a so-called Petit-Haiti Flea Market, an unsanitary landscape of chaos and filth with piles of garbage, potholed streets, puddles of dirty water, and pop music blasting at full volume.

"And what do you think is gonna happen?" Pierre Selvandieu asked his neighbor who was selling chickens from his coveted spot on the street corner. "It looks to me like they're gonna send us back to Haiti."

"You're crazy! We're fine here. Take that out of your head," replied Henri-Joseph, throwing up his arms as if he were warding off evil spirits. "More people keep coming in; yesterday they brought 15 girls and 30 boys through Dajabón to work. Five of the girls stayed here, you know, the others, they went to Boca Chica. And the boys, they'll be selling peanuts, cleaning windshields, and begging in the streets."

"But I have no papers, and they're going to ask me for them." Pierre was very distraught.

"Don't worry. I know a guy who can make you some. It costs 'une fortune' ... but I'll tell him and he'll hook you up, if you give him the money."

Pierre took in Henri-Joseph's proposition. He pondered how much it would cost him to obtain a false document in case he decided to get one, and the time it would take him to get the money together. Claude Philippe, the owner of the little used-clothing shop, deducted rent from his salary every month for a miserable little corner he shared with five others as a living space.

Pierre knew firsthand what it was to be a victim of deceit. When he was a kid he was brought here falling for the ruse he'd earn good money working at the sugar mill. And it was not so, he'd had to help his compatriots fill a daily sugar cane quota. He got paid whatever they paid him, not the dollars he'd been promised. He had already gone through deportation once, and did not want it to happen a second time. His precarious physical condition would not allow him to endure the truck ride, much less live in a place where there was nothing; where it was all over.

"No, I'll wait. I'm gonna get real papers so I can stay."

****

32

Thanks to Marcel's mentorship and fatherly guidance, Gabriel was able to discover the heart of the Haitian reality and got to intimately know the people who would play a key role in Haiti's social and economic reconstruction and development based on Marcel's model which promoted civic action.

"I will miss all our meetings and conversations so much," said Gabriel, looking sadly at Marcel. Marcel was driving his Camry towards Jimaní. They would say goodbye in Malpasse, and then Gabriel would cross the border to his hometown and country.

The time had passed very quickly, bringing with it the date set for Gabriel to return to the Dominican Republic and resume the life he had left when he took a year's sabbatical in Haiti. He had said a warm goodbye to Marie Thérèse, and they had agreed to stay in close touch.

"Yes, I'll miss you too. I have so appreciated your company and the opportunity you've given me to show you my country. I, through you, have also learned a lot about your country, our only neighbor, and that there are many good people like you in the Dominican Republic. I've always been deeply touched by your genuine interest in our troubles, and I am honored with your friendship." Marcel took his eyes off the road for a second to gaze at Gabriel.

"Likewise, Marcel. Thank you so much for what you've done for me. You're a truly outstanding man." Gabriel meant to say more, but the words didn't come out.

"I wanted you to see in everything I taught you the real political, economic, and social reasons behind the situations we have here. Do you remember that tense situation we witnessed a few days ago at one of the border crossings? I want you to keep two things in mind about it; First, that it was a provocation by design to fuel antagonistic feelings between Haitians and Dominicans. We should avoid these types of provocations at all costs. Second, and this is the most important, people must know the history of their country and learn from its lessons in order not to repeat them; that is a law of life. If you don't learn, you fail. That's part of the reason why we're currently finding ourselves back in colonial times, but in reverse," Marcel indicated.

"What do you mean?"

"Well, in colonial times, in 1767, when Haiti was the Pearl of the Antilles for its economic wealth, and we were considered the richest and most powerful colony in the world, meanwhile, on the other side of the same island, the Spanish colony, abandoned and forgotten by Spain, languished in poverty. Because of our economic power, there arose a feeling of superiority over the poor Spanish whites who lived in the eastern part of the island, coming here to the western part of the island to sell their livestock to us. Well, now the situation has reversed; many Dominicans are looking down disparagingly on Haitians in their poverty.

"Forgive me for interrupting, but most countries feel like that."

"I agree with you, but we know that for us, the rejection of other countries had historical reasons: the independence of the country, the abolition of slavery, and the declaration of equal rights and freedom. However, what we saw the other day between Haitians and Dominicans in Dajabón should be a wake-up call for Dominicans to look in the mirror we share. It must be done, in spite of the pain, because the Dominican Republic is walking down the same path that led us into misfortune; if the Dominican Republic continues to weaken its institutions and its citizens become apathetic about government mismanagement and corruption, it will end up like Haiti."

"Well, maybe things will change with the new government."

"Do you really think so?" questioned Marcel, looking askance at Gabriel. "The party in power uses the state's resources to stay in power. The individual actors may change, but the ideological machinery is the same, so the Dominican people will continue to play out the same drama as we have, perhaps even worse, I would say."

"I'd like to give them the benefit of the doubt," said Gabriel.

"I respect that, Gabriel, but my duty as your friend is to show you the truth about the Haitian reality, so that you will keep it in mind when you do whatever you decide to do in your country. Haiti is as it is, not just because it was isolated from the international community from its very beginnings, but also because of the power vacuum that emerged when our nation emerged, a vacuum that led to political instability and the rapid depletion of its resources due to the onerous indebtedness imposed by France in exchange for our independence, situations that greatly weakened the state and its institutions over time. All this led to impunity, corruption, a social apathy over the external interference in our affairs that in turn, led to our dependence on it; an interference that is keeping Haiti on its knees as a failed state because keeping Haiti subjugated is beneficial to hegemonic interests."

Once more, Marcel took his eyes off the road to gauge Gabriel's reaction to his words. Gabriel was absorbed in thought, his eyes fixed on the dashboard.

"Do you see the parallels? Do you see what can happen in the Dominican Republic if its leaders continue to act the way they're acting now? They will turn your country into another failed state, creating the perfect excuse for another foreign military intervention."

"I certainly do see the parallels; but what, in your mind, are the solutions to all these problems? And I'm not even including all the illegal activities that are having such a negative impact on both our societies. The authorities of both countries are fully responsible for not enforcing the controls and penalties in our laws."

"Do not think I'm joking or mocking you, because I'm not. But what is needed to solve the problems of public administration is going back to the basics; the government has to apply the same discipline and organization a regular person has to use to manage a household; that is, it must manage and organize itself with consistency and discipline, adhere to a budget in order to ensure the responsible and prudent use of money and other resources, control expenses, and have a plan for building savings, and the fair distribution of tax obligations and responsibilities for the common good of all, not just a select few. What do you say about that?"

"You're right, and thanks for another of your 'nutshell summaries' before I go, Marcel," chuckled Gabriel. Marcel joined in the laughter, his heart warmed with Gabriel's sincerity.

In Malpasse, Marcel parked the car a few meters from where crowds of Haitians were gathering in front of the border gate. He got out of the car and looked at his compatriots laden with merchandise. Gabriel also stepped out of the car and stood beside Marcel, appreciating the image for the last time. His heart ached with sorrow when the border opened and he saw the river of people begin to flow into Jimaní.

"Marcel, we'll keep in touch, you know you have a home on the other side," Gabriel murmured, his eyes tearing.

"You have a home here as well. You know you can always count on me." Marcel caught Gabriel in a bear hug like the one they gave each other in Cap-Haïtien after their first adventure together on the Dominican border, when their friendship deepened. The silence bore eloquent witness to the affection and admiration they felt for each other.

****

33

Gabriel was filled with mixed feelings as he crossed the border. He was happy to be home again, but at the same time, he felt a yearning to be back with the friends he'd shared a year with in Haiti. As he made his way home, he thought of the relativity of time; it seemed as if a century had passed since his life in Santo Domingo and yet, the year he had spent in Haiti felt like a few seconds.

He felt strange when he reached the doorstep of his childhood home: that nest Matilde had created for the two of them by herself, after the death of his father, a father he could only vaguely remember, but who still somehow felt close to him thanks to the photos Matilde had always kept on the walls. Gabriel sat in the living room to contemplate one in particular, where he was sitting on his father's lap.

Oh, how I wish you were on this plane, Dad. I'd like to tell you about my experience in Haiti, about the friendships I made there, but especially about Marcel. From everything Mom used to tell me about you, I keep getting the impression that the two of you have a lot in common. In these circumstances we need people like you two more than ever ... people with integrity and vision.

Gabriel closed his eyes, trying to imagine his father, imagine interacting with him. He concentrated on his breathing and began to meditate. He asked quietly to be shown the direction he needed to take in his life from this point. He meditated for thirty minutes, and when he opened his eyes, he grabbed his cell phone and dialed Matilde's number. The call went straight to her voicemail.

"Mom, I'm back home. I know you're busy. I can't wait to see you when you come home from work. Sending you a big hug. I love you, Mom."

He got up from the couch and went straight to his old bedroom. There, he sat at the desk Matilde bought him when he was six to study and do his homework. A smile touched his lips when he remembered how big that office desk seemed to him the first time it was placed in the room. He looked for a piece of paper in the top drawer, and of course, a sheaf of paper was lying there. He shook his head at how Matilde had always kept things exactly as they were, as if no time had passed. Wasn't it always that way with parents? Even when their children grow up, they still consider them their precious babies. He grabbed a piece of paper and a pen, and began to write out his action plan.

****

When it was almost time for Matilde to arrive home, Gabriel set the small kitchen table, put the *asopao* stew she had in the refrigerator in a pot to simmer, and went to the living room where he sat to read the newspaper, waiting for her arrival. The sound of the key in the door jolted him back to reality, and he leapt up and stood before the door to greet her.

"Gabriel! You're finally home!" Matilde threw herself into her son's embrace, crying and laughing, feeling a mother's joy and relief that her child was safe and sound. She stood apart from him for a moment to take a good look at him, and frenetically hugged and kissed him.

"Mom, I was just a few miles away," Gabriel said, trying to reassure her.

"No, for me you were in the middle of hell considering the condition Haiti has been in since the earthquake, the cholera outbreak, and everything ... " Matilde paused to take her purse off her right shoulder and laid it on the coffee table in the center of the living room. "Now you're going to tell me everything you did."

"I'll tell you all about it while we have dinner. I found the *asopao* in the fridge and already put it in a pot to simmer."

"Okay, but you'd better tell me all the details and don't leave anything out. Look how skinny you are! Did you get sick over there?"

"No, not at all. I walked a lot, and worked very hard. Rest assured your prayers were heard. God protected me, and put me in touch with angels who guided and helped me the whole time I was there." Gabriel kissed the top of Matilde's head as they headed down the hallway into the kitchen.

****

34

Gabriel went back to Santo Domingo after spending a week with Matilde, because she had needed a few repairs around the house. As soon as he reached the city, he called Don Emilio Martínez Durán, his boss and mentor, to let him know that he was back, and ready to return to work whenever he was instructed to do so. Don Emilio invited him to his house on Saturday night in order to talk about his experience in Haiti.

"What a joy to have you back home," greeted Don Emilio. "Come in, come in, Sandra will be joining us in a few minutes. I want to hear all about your sabbatical."

"I've been wanting to talk to you, too. You were on my mind the whole time I was there." Gabriel presented Don Emilio a bottle of wine he had brought for the occasion and chocolates for Doña Sandra. Don Emilio placed them on the coffee table in the living room, and they both took a seat.

"So, first of all ... tell me what impressed you most?"

"The devastation ... and it looks as if the earthquake had hit only yesterday. There are no words to describe the magnitude of the tragedy. But I was equally impressed by the resilience and kindness of the Haitian people, especially the people I spent time with, including Marcel Vincent, a professor at the National University, and Marie Thérèse Cadet, a young woman of the Haitian diaspora who'd come back from Canada to help her people in the aftermath of the earthquake. Marcel took me under his wing, and taught me the reality of Haiti and how it will rise from the rubble."

"Gabriel! How nice to have you back!" cried Doña Sandra as she came into the living room.

Gabriel and Don Emilio stood up, and Gabriel hugged and kissed Doña Sandra.

"Gabriel was telling me that he met a university professor who gave him guidance while he was in Haiti, and that the country is still as shattered as it was when the earthquake occurred," Don Emilio informed Doña Sandra.

Don Emilio and Gabriel returned to their armchairs once doña Sandra settled down on the couch, and Gabriel continued with his story.

"I was working with an organization fighting against the abuse and forced labor being perpetrated on the *restaveks*, Haitian children whose mothers are sending them to live in Port-au-Prince so that they will have the life they cannot give them, but who end up as slaves, unfortunately. I also got involved with Marcel and his collaborators in their social initiative to promote free public education for all Haitians, and I was also involved in activities promoting private initiatives, investment, and microenterprise as a way of encouraging economic development among the most impoverished groups of Haitian society. Marcel has the conviction that these efforts will generate the change of mentality and culture he believes will be necessary for Haiti to re-emerge from the rubble and rise along with the Dominican Republic as the mythological two-headed dragon, as he says."

"Interesting! " exclaimed Don Emilio.

"Please tell us more over dinner, Gabriel, it's ready." Doña Sandra smiled and stood up, and Gabriel and Don Emilio followed her into the dining room.

"We were talking about a two-headed dragon," Doña Sandra commented as they sat down at the table. "I like that image of Hispaniola a lot more than the one people like to use of the conjoined twins, who give me the impression to punch each other all the time, don't you think?"

Her observation caused the men to laugh in agreement.

"As negative an image as that of the Dominican Republic as a marriage without divorce," added Don Emilio.

"Yes, well, the image of the two-headed dragon is striking, but also significant," Gabriel pointed out. "According to Greek mythology, the two-headed dragon has the gifts of regeneration and healing of wounds. Which are what the two nations need to coexist in peace and harmony."

"True," said Don Emilio and Doña Sandra in unison.

"After hearing everything that Marcel had to say, and seeing everything he was doing, I have no doubt that he's right. In Haiti, the birth rate has tripled since the earthquake. That means the country will undergo a demographic growth that will impact the entire island in the future. Now is the time to bring about the change of culture and mindset that Haiti needs, and this can only be achieved through education and economic development. Truly, this is really what the island needs. It's just what I formulated 30 years ago when I proposed an economic confederation and a common market. Do you remember how I talked about that in class?"

"Of course. The new government intends to build this binational market; unbelievable, though, the years we've spent planning it. There's always been some sort of issue coming up. Amazing!"

"I know, I went there to verify what I already knew, that the bureaucracy weighs more than people's needs, that in this country laws are enacted and agreements signed all the time but not enforced, just as with the royal decrees passed in colonial times that were obeyed in word but not upheld in deed. The migratory chaos we have is the result of years of neglect and complacency on the part of government and law enforcement officials on both sides of the border."

"I think our country got messed up when morals and civics stopped being taught in our schools," said Doña Sandra as she tucked into a piece of chocolate cake with vanilla ice cream.

"Yes, the lack of education and civic and moral values is destroying our families and therefore, our society. Training and technology alone are not enough to educate people," added Don Emilio.

Gabriel sighed in agreement. "I plan to get back to work as soon as possible, of course, but I also want to introduce Marcel's model here; I want to see more citizen involvement in our society."

"So are you going to jump into politics?" questioned Don Emilio, looking Gabriel in the eyes. "It's the only thing left for you to do, and if you run for office, I feel you would do very well."

"No, Don Emilio. Not at all. I haven't even been thinking about that. I believe we are more in need of good role models on the ground, actions at the grassroots level to convince people we can have the nation our founders Duarte, Sánchez, and Mella dreamed of, and defend our sovereignty, our nationality through the commitment of our citizens on a day-to-day basis, not just on national holidays and not just making gestures to our neighbors in times of crisis."

"That's very good, Gabriel, you've come back at just the right time to provide some innovative solutions for the heated disagreements afflicting our society," noted Doña Sandra.

"Yes, we need you back at the office now more than ever," Don Emilio commented in a serious tone. "The Haitian immigrant situation is getting explosive and is dividing the nation. There are those who see and applaud the contributions

Haitians have made in many sectors of the economy, and there are those who see only an invasion of the country and Dominican displacement."

"Because of what I saw in Haiti, I am sure Haitian migration to the Dominican Republic will remain at high levels. Their need is what is pushing them to come here. It's a real shame."

"Then, I'm counting on you to be at the office on Monday." Don Emilio gazed at Gabriel, smiling.

"Of course, Don Emilio, it is an honor and a pleasure to work with you. And I thank you both for your invitation to dinner tonight and your kind gestures. I must not wear out my welcome, though; it is time for me to go," said Gabriel, bidding them goodbye with the affection of a son towards his parents. "Good night. And thank you both so very much."

****

35

"You didn't say if you wanted the papers," Henri-Joseph commented one morning to Pierre Selvandieu as they disappeared from their customary posts on the sidewalk at the sight of a National Police officer walking down the street toward them, watching the area.

"No, I don't want those kinds of papers. I don't want problems," answered Pierre nervously, tightening the grip on the cane he used to walk.

"And what do you think is gonna happen? If you have papers, the police won't bother you; papers that say you were born here, that you're a Dominican."

"What kind of papers does this guy make?"

"IDs, or birth certificates that say you were born here, and if the officials says so, well, they're the authority. You do it to stay here, not to deny Haiti."

"And how much does it cost, exactly? You never said."

"Yes, I did tell you, it costs a fortune ... 10,000 Dominican pesos, but hey, nobody's gonna bother you." Henri-Joseph looked closely at Pierre trying to read his thoughts.

Pierre Selvandieu's heart began racing. All of a sudden, memories of the past rushed back to assault him yet again; these ghosts chased him all the time, but he refused to bend despite the torment. Bodily pain was the only type of pain Pierre was willing to accept and tolerate, because it reminded him every day of how lucky he was to be alive.

"You've got a spirit riding your head! You aren't here!" Henri-Joseph exclaimed, concerned with Pierre's sudden distraction.. "Everybody's doing it ..."

"No *loa* is riding my head!" Pierre muttered, making his way back from his memories. "It's this physical pain that doesn't stop." And with that, Pierre withdrew into the used-clothing shop, walking very slowly, leaning hard on his cane, resolving to keep working hard every day and keep trusting that the spirits would continue to save him from danger, as they had done in the past.

Inside the little shop, Pierre kept thinking of Henri-Joseph and others like him who constantly sought out clients for the mafia, immigrants desperate for documents, food, safety, a place to live. He wondered how much of a cut Henri-Joseph would get from the 10,000 pesos charged per document. Likewise, he wondered how much money he got for all the newcomers he brought to the mafia for prostitution and begging in the streets.

****

The rampant document fraud, including birth certificate falsifications and alterations occurring in many vital records offices and in hospitals along the border and in other regions of the country, as well as fake voter registration cards and national identity cards, reached such alarming proportions that the Constitutional Court was prompted to vigorously defend Dominican nationality and identity with Ruling No. 168 of September 23, 2013, adding yet more controversy to the Haitian immigration situation.

The country's population was divided on the ruling. Some were in favor of the court's decision, while others were completely against it because of the legal, political, and economic repercussions the court's position would generate at national and international levels.

At the Dominican chancellery, and in every other part of the country, politicians, legal experts, and professionals from different fields of knowledge analyzed the content and scope of the 147-page decision, including the viewpoints of the two dissenting judges.

"This is truly a landmark ruling," commented Don Emilio to the lawyers of the legal department of the chancellery. "The judges of the Constitutional Court have drawn a clear line in the sand of our legal framework regarding our national sovereignty, who is to be considered a migrant, and the guidelines the Central Electoral Board and Office of Immigration should follow in establishing legal mechanisms for the regularization of migrants and the issuance of identity documents; and therefore, solve the human drama of these individuals. My hat is off to these magistrates, who with this ruling have forced the executive branch to assume the responsibility it has so long ignored with regard to regularizing the immigration crisis."

"Indeed, the ruling is thorough and very weighty. In the 101 pages that make up the actual decision, since the remaining 46 contain the opinions of the two dissenting judges, the judges of the Constitutional Court have conducted a thorough study of administrative law, comparative law, and constitutional law to support their position, as a court of last resort in constitutional matters and fundamental rights like the right to citizenship and national identity. With this ruling, the Court declared its jurisdiction to hear the appeal of the Trial Court of Monte Plata's decision, establishing a general rule for similar cases under the *erga omnes* effect its own decisions have," Gabriel replied.

"Certainly." added Pablo Cabrera, another attorney of the legal department. "Its decisions are opposable but binding on all branches of the government as the court serving as the guardian and guarantor of constitutional and fundamental rights. Now those matters are clearly defined, as Don Emilio very eloquently put it."

"That's correct," said Gabriel, "the ruling vindicates the sovereign right of the Dominican state to give the political right of citizenship, but at the same time, and here is the point that detractors and critics don't see, the decision protects the fundamental rights of people improperly registered as Dominican in the Office of Vital Records as children of temporary Haitian residents, but also the rights of other people in the same situation, when the Court instructed the Office of Immigration to grant a special temporary permit to them within 10 days to regularize their situation, while the validity or invalidity of the original birth certificate was determined by the local court. In my opinion, this provision puts an end to any misinterpretation of the retroactive review of records from 1929 to 2008, when the Book of Births of children of foreign non-resident mothers was put into effect, leaving thousands of people without documentation and without citizenship."

"The first thing the chancellery has to make clear to the public is that there will be no such situation any more," noted Don Emilio. "Haitians have *ius sanguinis* so that they will not be left without a nationality if the Dominican state voids a document that was proven to be falsified or improperly granted, because Dominican nationality did not belong to them; but the second thing we must emphasize is the principle that illegality cannot lead to legality."

"This ruling has been harshly criticized," Gabriel added. "However, it's the same position the Supreme Court has assumed since 1929 when serving as a court of cassation or when it served as our Constitutional Court before the Constitutional Court was created in 2010: that a temporary resident in the Dominican territory does not have the right to Dominican nationality. In other words, even if a foreigner has been living in the Dominican Republic for 20 years, he doesn't have the right to citizenship if he doesn't hold legal permanent residency; therefore, a migrant in a non-regularized state is a temporary resident, even if he has been born here."

"I particularly loved this innovative concept of the 'margin of appreciation' or the state's discretion as a member-state of the international community to introduce limitations to rights without violating fundamental rights," Pablo Cabrera commented.

"Yes, I like the new point regarding the principle of the *inter comunis* effects of the Constitutional Court's ruling, where the same decision may be made in similar cases and situations along the lines of what it has handed down." Gabriel sat on his desk with a copy of the ruling in his hands.

" I do not agree with the Constitutional Court, or with you all,"said Angel Báez, the only attorney who had remained silent up to this point. "My opinion is with that of the dissenting judges."

"Well, you have the right to disagree, of course, Angel; your position only reflects the sentiments of the Court and of the Dominican people. Our office is no exception to the rule. It is in line with the purity of the law. However, that's not what's at stake here, but national sovereignty and outside interference."

Don Emilio stood up, leaving his copy of the ruling on his desk. He had been looking for a way to address the matter and settle it once and for all with the tact and respect his colleague deserved.

"Angel, what all Dominicans must understand is that the decision by the Constitutional Court has the same force as a law enacted by Congress, so, like it or not, whether we agree with it or not, it must be applied and must be observed. Gentlemen, we will be very busy with this ruling, which tries to regularize the condition of those who have obtained documents in an irregular manner, including Dominicans who have acted illegally. The sad thing is that this ruling will probably be used against the country, where vested interests will give it undertones it does not have because it suits their interests to solve a geopolitical problem by using us."

****

36

Within 90 days from the notification of Ruling 168 of the Constitutional Court to the Central Electoral Board and General Office of Immigration, the Dominican executive branch presented the National Regularization Plan for Foreigners under Decree 327-13. The program would last 18 months and would be carried out in two phases.

The first phase would run from December 1, 2013 to May 31, 2014. It was intended to set up the legal structure and institutions for carrying out the Plan, and for preparing the qualification requirements that persons interested in regularization had to meet. The second phase, which would run from June 1, 2014 to May 31, 2015, was for the issuance of documents to irregular residents who were accepted into the plan.

Thousands of people, most of them Haitians, practically overran the General Immigration Office, the Haitian Embassy in Santo Domingo, and the Haitian consulates in other regions of the country to regularize their immigration status in response to the national government's campaign encouraging them to register.

"The line never budges an inch, and then when you finally reach the official, he says you have to go back. I don't understand!" a Haitian woman complained to one of her compatriots waiting his turn in line.

"I've been here in line since last night. Look at the guy right there," explained an older gentleman to a young man behind him, "that guy walking up and down collecting money was saying he gets to go ahead of you, he paid for his spot. He's crazy if he thinks I'm gonna pay him the money I need for my document!"

"This is real bad. Look, I've been waiting a long time with my three children, and nothing happens. I've been carrying the two youngest ones for hours. That's not right. I need to feed the older one and keep him close by so he doesn't run off. Explain to me how I'm gonna hang on to him too?" complained a Haitian woman with three children, the oldest appearing to be four judging by his height, while the two she carried appeared to be a couple of months old and one year old.

The endless queue of applicants became part of the landscape around the General Office of Immigration. Haitians set up camp on Calle Rafael Damirón; they ate and slept in the area, creating overcrowding and unsanitary conditions.

Haitian communities all across the Dominican Republic turned into hornets' nests. The comments and opinions of Haitians reflected their abject fears about an uncertain future and a long and complicated process they did not quite understand.

****

Pierrre Selvandieu expected to be one of the 11,000 Haitians who, according to his country's ambassador, would get Haitian documentation and thus be legal residents in the Dominican Republic. He was one of the first to show up at the Haitian Embassy in Santo Domingo to register in the National Regularization Plan for Foreigners. He endured an epically long line, and most of all, the severe pain that had tortured him since he was rescued from under the rubble of the Port-au-Prince Market five days after the earthquake; now, he was faced another type of torture, the mental kind: whether he would receive his documentation or not.

"The spirits won't forsake me now, they're gonna give me my paper," Pierre said to Henri-Joseph when they had heard comments on the news about the Haitian government's inability to provide documentation to their people.

"You better think about where to go, because they're gonna deport you if you don't go. That's it!" Henri-Joseph advised his neighbor pragmatically.

"No, I told the consul when he interviewed me that I didn't come here on my own; I was brought to a hospital here. He saw the bad shape I'm in. I can't go back. He told me everything would be fine, that I was gonna get my passport." Pierre stood firm in that conviction, feeling in his innermost being that the spirits were protecting him.

Henri-Joseph shook his head, thinking how stubborn and ignorant Pierre was, refusing to see the reality that awaited him.

****

37

"Gentlemen, the bomb has gone off, just as we expected," Don Emilio commented to his colleagues when he returned to the chancellery early in the afternoon. He had spent the morning with the foreign affairs minister in the office of the Dominican president analyzing the decision of the Inter-American Court of Human Rights of October 28, 2014. "Never in my entire career have I seen an international institution adopt such a disrespectful position of interference as this one, ordering the Dominican state to deny its sovereignty and violate its constitution and its laws."

The other lawyers in the department gathered around Don Emilio to hear the details.

"According to the Inter-American Court of Human Rights, the Dominican state disregarded and violated the human rights obligations it had assumed when it signed the Convention on Human Rights and accepted the jurisdictional authority of the Inter-American Court of Human Rights." Don Emilio sat on his desk, overwhelmed with fatigue. He felt as if he had been riding a roller coaster since early that morning.

"We knew the judges of the Court would rule like they did," commented Angel Báez pragmatically.

"You are absolutely right, Angel, it was expected. What was unexpected about this decision is that it did not give 'recommendations', but rather demanded and set up deadlines for the Dominican state to issue identity documents and grant citizenship to the people affected by the case, and invalidate government investigations or civil and criminal court proceedings for the registration of these people's documents." Emilio took a deep breath. "And, of course, the Court ordered us to pay them compensation. But, to top it all off, it's the audacity of demanding the state to strike down Ruling No 168 of the Constitutional Court and immigration laws intended to deny citizenship to people born in our territory based on ancestry or origin and the irregular situation of their parents. To ensure this decision is obeyed, the Court ordered the Dominican state to provide within a year from the announcement of the Court's ruling, evidence of what it has done in this regard; and it went even further, in emphasizing that full compliance with the ruling was part of the requirement."

"Indeed, Don Emilio. This opinion is a gross interference. In my opinion, it's another manipulative ploy to force the Dominican Republic to assimilate a migrant population any nation wants to receive. It is obvious they want to prevent the government from going ahead with the National Regularization Plan for Foreigners," said Gabriel.

"That's right, but they're not going to get away with it. Gentlemen, we have to prepare to defend the sovereignty of the Dominican state, which obviously is the duty of the president of the country, " Don Emilio concluded vehemently.

****

Gabriel and his colleagues worked at the chancellery well into the evening, preparing the defense of the Dominican state, writing legal arguments to rebut the ruling of the Inter-American Court of Human Rights, paragraph by paragraph.

When Gabriel left the office, he was tired and his legs felt heavy. He decided to take a walk through Mirador del Sur, one of the biggest greenspaces in the city of Santo Domingo, built along Avenida Mirador del Sur. He thought the stroll would physically and mentally refresh him.

The irony of life … here I am taking the same evening stroll Dr. Balaguer used to, thought Gabriel, as he walked along. He recalled the work written by the Dominican

Republic's deceased president, The Island in Reverse, which formulated the Haitian problem and discussed the peaceful invasion of the country.

Gabriel, like President Balaguer, had a photographic memory, so he could see in his mind the paragraphs of the IACHR's ruling that disturbed him the most. Some of the sentences were downright sinister. *Hegemonic interests are relentless. How long will the Dominican state withstand their pressures?*

Suddenly, another paragraph appeared in his mind: "Since the early nineties, the Inter-American Commission has been receiving reports of institutionalized racial discrimination in the Dominican Republic against persons of Haitian descent or perceived as such, which has particularly affected the granting of citizenship and has led to their deportation and expulsion, among other situations ."

There are some things that never change. Marcel, you're right. If we don't wake up, we will pay dearly for it. The Court is using the old trick of racism and discrimination against us.

"Divide and conquer … that was the maxim of Niccolò Machiavelli," Gabriel said aloud, stopping briefly in his tracks when he heard the sound of his voice. Then he began to walk quickly in the opposite direction, wanting to be in the tranquility of his apartment to chat with his good friend Marcel Vincent.

****

The stroll had whetted his appetite. Gabriel stopped at a pizzeria and ordered a medium-sized pizza to go. While eating the pizza in his apartment, he thought of Matilde; she wouldn't consider it a real dinner. He smiled to himself.

After he finished 'dinner' and listened to the news, he showered and waited for the right time to call Marcel. Sometimes calls to Haiti did not go through, or reception was quite spotty.

"Good evening, Marcel," said Gabriel as soon as Marcel picked up.

"How nice to hear from you, Gabriel, how are you?"

"Well, a little concerned. I don't know if you're aware of today's news regarding the ruling of the Inter-American Court of Human Rights."

"Today, I had some commitments away from Port-au-Prince, so I didn't keep up with the news. What's up?"

"Truly, the only thing that's really new is how they word things; but behind the words they're always insisting on the same thing, to provoke conflict."

"What do you mean?"

"To whip up the racism that supposedly exists among Dominicans against Haitians. I won't ignore reality. I recognize there are sectors of Dominican society that strongly reject Haitians, but it's not because of the color of their skin."

"As you say, it's nothing new, and as you know, rejection is not exclusive to Dominicans. That's why I'm working so hard to promote education in Haiti; it's the only way to eradicate the ignorance and illiteracy afflicting my people. And as we've discussed, this is the new way hegemonic nations isolate us today. They want us to be undesirable and to stay as 'ungovernable' as ever, of course, to control us."

"Then, I'm going to give you a 'nutshell summary' of just how far the interference of hegemonic interests has gone," said Gabriel, a tone of sarcasm in his voice.

"I am all ears."

"The Inter-American Court has demanded that we violate our own constitution and laws because they are not in agreement with the provisions of the Inter-American Human Rights Convention; the ruling has established deadlines to implement measures of compliance."

"The ruling has a political undertone." Marcel commented. "And I agree with you, the Court wants to stop the regularization of foreigners while it still has a chance. And you can count on the fact, Gabriel, that the Haitian Government won't be immune to such pressure, either. They're going to push Haiti's back against the wall to obstruct the process, because what matters is to maintain the status quo, anarchy. Am I clear? In a stormy sea, there are bound to be good pickings. "

"That's what I was thinking earlier. 'Divide and conquer,' Machiavelli's old maxim. They want to keep us fighting like cats and dogs to achieve their goal. I'll tell you one thing, if I were the Dominican president, the nation wouldn't be subject to the jurisdiction of the IACHR on this matter."

"It's possible to do that. The Dominican state must be firm and make perfectly clear that it will not adopt an attitude of servility and sacrifice its sovereignty on the IACHR's political altar. But it has to tread carefully because I don't think the Dominican Republic can escape the hegemonic yoke as other countries from the region did. We can't lose sight of the fact that Puerto Plata is located less than 1,500 miles from Florida. In other words, Haiti and the Dominican Republic are in the United States' back yard. They'll always have us on a short leash. However, powerful countries shouldn't forget that with globalization, we all live in glass houses now, and if they throw a stone, even with their control of the media, they won't be able to block the people's access to and participation in the virtual network that is so influential today. Nowadays, we are all 'exposed.' In my opinion, Gabriel, I think the Dominican government will keep feeling the noose tighten behind the scenes, even though the state is defending its sovereignty, as it should. This tug-of-war has gone on forever."

"They're strangling us economically, and as we Dominicans say, 'they'll shut off the water and the power' if we don't obey."

"You hit the nail on the head with that analogy, Gabriel. It's perfect."

"It's a popular saying here. But, yes, that's how our relations with these powerful interests are. "

"Unless we are all aware of reality and work together to bring about positive change."

"Of course. Thanks, Marcel, for listening to me and for your friendship. You don't know how good I feel when I chat with you. Please give my best regards to Marie Thérèse."

"I will, with pleasure. She's an exceptional young woman. When we talk, she mentions you often. I think she likes you very much, if you know what I mean."

"Yes, I do. I think she's pretty special too. Marcel, don't ever forget how much I value your friendship, and I'm always happy to talk to you. Good night; see you soon."

****

38

A year and two months after it handed down the famous Ruling No. 168 of September 23, 2013, the Constitutional Court again made history, this time with regard to an appeal filed in 2005 arguing the unconstitutionality of the document signed in 1999 by the Dominican president accepting the jurisdiction of the Inter-American Court of Human Rights. The Constitutional Court accepted the appeal and declared the document unconstitutional in Ruling No. 256 of November 5, 2014.

As with its previous ruling, the Constitutional Court's decision provoked much controversy and debate in Dominican society and among legal experts, and deepened the fault line between those who supported and those who disagreed with the first ruling. A similar division also emerged within the Court with four judges dissenting.

After Gabriel and his colleagues analyzed the ruling at the office, as was customary when they worked as a team, he sat down at his desk and began working on his own projects. Evening approached, and as he headed down the main hall of the chancellery to go home, he ran into Don Emilio.

"Thank you for serving as the moderator at this morning's meeting. Our analysis of the ruling looked like a televised panel discussion," Don Emilio commented discreetly.

"Well, we have some colleagues with a strong background in international law, so they think like the dissenting judges, who are correct as far as the purity of the law goes. However, they do not see that the IACHR is seriously overreaching and acting repressively, deciding in accordance with certain political interests that, in this case, are demanding we change our constitutional laws which are protected by the Inter-American Convention on Human Rights," pointed out Gabriel.

"Of course, the behavior of the Court is generating tensions and rifts between member states of the Convention regarding this matter, as has happened with other member- states. In principle, the Court must be impartial and rule only on matters related to the Convention," said Don Emilio, shaking his head at the political position of the IACHR.

"It's a pity the IACHR is acting like this. What matters is that the Dominican Constitutional Court made it crystal clear that any decision made by the executive branch of an international scope must be approved by Congress as established in our Constitution, which never happened when the president signed that document of acceptance of the IACHR's jurisdiction in 1999."

"Likewise, the Dominican Constitutional Court recognized the right of the Dominican state to adhere to any agreement of cooperation, regional integration or the protection of fundamental rights, so long as they observed constitutional procedure and constitutional law," Don Emilio commented, supporting the decision of Dominican judges on a delicate matter of paramount importance to Dominican diplomacy.

"Once again, the Constitutional Court has defended our sovereignty," Gabriel said.

"Too bad I have some family commitments, otherwise we could continue this conversation at home. We'll have a chance to talk." Don Emilio winked at Gabriel, placing his hand on his former pupil's shoulder in an affectionate goodbye.

****

39

There was a sudden burst of activity among Haitians who had not yet registered with the National Regularization Plan for Foreigners when the deadline for the program's end began approaching. Many of them returned to Haiti on their own, provoking an immediate reaction from the Haitian president.

Gabriel's cell phone began ringing as he walked into his apartment at the end of the workday. He smiled when he saw Marcel's name pop up on the screen, and picked up with an eager hello.

"Good evening, Gabriel, I hope it isn't too late to call you."

"No, you called at just the right time, Marcel. I was just thinking about you. I think we're about to face another political storm." Gabriel plopped his briefcase on the living room sofa and sat down beside it.

"Indeed, that's the reason I called you. Our media has already been reporting our president's position, which in my opinion is pretty belligerent. He stated that Haiti would not accept massive repatriations from the Dominican government that might destabilize us."

"It's a shame that after all the help Haiti has received and continues to receive from the Dominican Republic, the Haitian President comes out with a stance like that, throwing fuel on the fire of the immigration situation. The Dominican government is not interested in destabilizing Haiti. That would intensify this human drama even more; we'd be destroying with our feet what we've built with our hands."

"You and I get it because we are willing to rise above the circumstances in order to seek the common good, but there are many who are blind, carried away by reasoning based on premises that are completely wrong, and they're reacting accordingly."

"I know. And speaking of the Haitian government, how are things progressing with you over there?"

"Very slowly. There are other issues that must come second, behind the agenda of those who put our president in power. The important thing is not to give up, to keep on working to achieve our goals. One does not plant seeds, then remove the soil the next day to see if they're germinating ... Well, I'll leave you to your rest. Hang in there."

"Thank you, Marcel, I wish you the same. Good night."

****

When the second phase of the National Regularization Plan for Foreigners had ended, the Dominican president met with his cabinet to evaluate the results of the plan and come up with follow-up measures.

"The chancellery is already working with the Haitian foreign affairs ministry on the protocol for repatriating the Haitians who didn't register under the Plan. We must avoid unnecessary crises. The Haitian president has already made his government's position very public with regard to the repatriations we can and cannot do. He insisted that Haiti will not receive 'Dominicans of Haitian descent,'" the Dominican foreign affairs minister stated, his brow creased with concern.

"This is a matter where everything's reduced to 'damned if you do, and damned if you don't.' It doesn't matter how hard we try to fix it, it seems to always end up without head or tail. They criticize the Plan, calling it a total failure, and the Dominican government is accused of deliberately imposing difficult requirements to prevent Haitians from being regularized, and the Haitian government of not providing passports to Haitian nationals who've paid for it." The minister of the interior and National Police was visibly uncomfortable with Dominican opinion leaders who constantly spoke out in the media to misinform the people.

"Indeed. We've received plenty of complaints about irregularities in certain business sectors aimed at hindering the regularization process, especially with respect to Haitians working in construction and irregularities on the part of the Haitian government with regard to regularizing Haitians working in the sugarcane industry. The Haitian government has apologized for it," noted the labor minister.

"Apology accepted," the Dominican president interrupted sarcastically, "but this problem must be solved as soon as possible. We Dominicans are going to blamed for it and we're the ones who are going to have to pay the piper regarding undocumented Haitians in the sugarcane sector."

"They can talk and say whatever they want, numbers do not lie. According to the latest nationwide immigration survey conducted by the National Bureau of Statistics with technical assistance from the United Nations Population Fund and the Delegation of the European Union, the total population of foreigners in the Republic had reached 524,632 people, of whom 458,233 were Haitian," the director general of immigration pointed out, his face shining with enthusiasm. "Thanks to the work of the Dominican government, we now know Haitians represent 96 percent of the 239,300 foreigners who registered in the Plan. For me, that's a success, considering all the limitations and challenges we had to face in executing the process with so many undocumented Haitians out there; actually, the vast majority of them. We've also taken biometric data from them and we are evaluating how to proceed in that regard."

"There will always be naysayers. Don't forget the allegations that the Haitian and Dominican governments were being paid by the mafia to accept new registrants in the Plan. Now that the deadline to participate in the Plan has passed, there will be accusations of human rights violations against the migrants who didn't make it into the Plan. It would be a smart move for our government to extend the deadline for those who were unable to complete the registration process," the attorney general opined.

"Yes, that would show the generosity and goodwill of the Dominican government in this delicate matter." The foreign affairs minister nodded in agreement with the attorney general's proposal.

The Dominican president, following the advice of his ministers, granted several grace periods to foreigners who had signed up with the Plan and who had entered the Dominican Republic prior to October 2011, but did not have all the required documents. The top priority at that time was to institutionalize the National Regularization Plan for Foreigners in order to determine the number of foreigners with legal residence and proceed with repatriating all foreigners without legal residence to their country of origin, whether they were of Haitian or any other nationality.

****

"Your Excellency, 4,850 Haitian immigrants have been left out of the National Regularization Plan for Foreigners," the director general of immigration reported to the Dominican president two weeks after the cabinet meeting had taken place. "We will begin repatriating them in August as the Haitian foreign ministry had agreed with our chancellery and our ministry of the interior and National Police."

"Make sure the budget department allocates the necessary resources for transportation, logistics, fuel and everything that is necessary for treating them with dignity and respect."

"Indeed, Your Excellency, we will follow the notification protocol that was agreed on with the Haitian government to receive its nationals at the Repatriation Management Center on the border, which has beds and bathrooms and have separate facilities for men and women."

"Needless to say, every single thing that is done should be properly documented to avoid unpleasant surprises later on." The president was signing documents, one after the other, as he spoke.

"Repatriations will be done through the towns of Elías Piña and Jimaní. We will send through an average of 250 people per day. As I said before, we will wait until the flow of Haitians returning voluntarily to Haiti decreases. They're afraid to lose what few possessions they've got in case they are detained."

"We must tread carefully. We're under enough pressure with rumors of possible mass repatriations circulating due to your department's purchase of a lot of new buses." The president looked up at the director general of immigration for a moment, then turned his attention to signing the last document he had on his desk. The director general understood that the audience was over.

"Before I leave, I'd also like to report, Your Excellency, that we will also repatriate 14 Hindus, 8 Cubans, 4 Iraqis, 2 Colombians, and 1 Dutch national who entered with passports as tourists, but who overstayed their visas to go to various destinations undocumented."

"Make sure that gets published in the newspapers," said the president, grabbing a black folder on the far right corner of his desk.

****

40

As soon as the Haitian Embassy made the official announcement that passports were to be issued to the 11,000 Haitians who registered in the Plan, Pierre Selvandieu left home in the early morning hours and headed directly there.

To his surprise, the line of was not as long as he'd expected. Pierre took his place in line and waited patiently for the hours to pass. When the embassy opened for business, the process of handing out the passports turned out to be as painfully slow as the process for registering in the Haitian Immigrant Identification and Documentation Program. But this did not bother him at all; the anticipation of having legal documentation erased all thoughts of inconvenience or discomfort.

"The information isn't in the computer so the papers aren't in order. They have to look and look for the papers to find them. But, here, I've got mine. I'll be fine now with a passport," said one Haitian to those still waiting in line, excitedly showing them his precious document.

But Pierre felt as if the earth had opened up to swallow him when he saw another compatriot come out of the Haitian Embassy empty-handed. Seized with despair, he asked the woman behind to him to hold his spot in line to go after the man.

"Wait, my friend!" shouted Pierre. The man came to a stop and turned around.

 "Are you okay?" the man asked Pierre, taking in Pierre's slow, painful steps as he leaned heavily on his cane. He gazed at him with concern.

"Yes, yes, I'm fine. Why don't you have your passport?"

"They just said I need to come back in three days, that today it was not my turn. So I say, well, I'll come back in three days."

Pierre nodded. He was physically exhausted by his efforts to catch up with the man;

the effects of his painkillers were beginning to wear off. He turned away, walked back to his place in line, thanked the lady who had held it for him, and waited for several more hours.

The adrenaline prodded him to remain erect as he approached the door to collect the document his country's government had promised to provide him. He went inside the office, and after enduring an agonizingly slow process, he was given a Haitian passport.

"I knew it, I knew it! Thank you, thank you!" Pierre repeated to the embassy's staff. He exited the Embassy crying and laughing, showing off his passport as if it were a great trophy to those still waiting in line.

"Look, look! I'm legal here now!"

****

Gabriel was in his apartment writing an essay on his computer about Dominican immigration policy and the progress being made in the implementation of the National Regularization Plan for Foreigners, which had been made possible thanks to the cooperation of the government, international agencies, and the private sector.

He wrote significant facts that he extracted from his research:

"The beneficiaries of the Plan now had a document that allowed them to circulate freely throughout the Dominican Republic without being deported. Authorities had to determine whether the identity card could be used to open a bank account, sign contracts, or register children who were born in the country. Those who had the card could be enrolled in the national social security system, although the government had not yet established a social protection strategy specifically for Haitian immigrants.

For most people who obtained the card, it was temporary and did not follow the immigration categories determined by Migration Law 285-04.

Meanwhile, the Immigrant Identification and Documentation Program executed by the Haitian government did not yield the expected results. The government had planned for 300,000 Haitians to receive passports, but only received 30,000 applications and granted 2,081 passports. The Haitian Inspector General alleged that there was a misappropriation of funds.

Haitian authorities had to resolve, effectively and quickly, the situation of its citizens living in the Dominican Republic."

Gabriel's fingers moved swiftly on his computer keyboard, reflecting the ideas that were seething in his head.

The Economic Impact of the National Regularization Plan for Foreigners on Haiti and the Dominican Republic. He wrote it as a title, and began to formulate questions that he posed to himself regarding the Plan's short- and long-term results.

Would it help both states work properly and therefore, strengthen their institutions?

Would it generate transparency and the regularization of formal and informal binational markets by establishing policies that encourage and facilitate commercial activity?

Would it encourage public and private investment by generating economic and social progress on the island?

Would it drive economic development in the border regions?

Would it produce a change in people's mindsets about Haitian immigration?

Gabriel stopped writing. He went to the kitchen to get a glass of water. He felt that he was burning inside. He knew the challenges Haiti and the Dominican Republic had to overcome in order to get a positive answer to all those questions. He emptied the glass quickly and set it on the kitchen counter, gripping the edge of it tightly.

"Yes, we *can* accomplish it," he said aloud, as if he were convincing and encouraging himself at once. "If we are all united against bureaucratic red tape and the elite minorities who are disrespecting the law and promoting corruption, chaos, and division to their advantage to the detriment of other citizens. We can achieve this, if we all reject our old patterns of behavior and act as dignified citizens committed to civic values.

"I hope the institutionalization of the National Regularization Plan for Foreigners recognizes Haitians' contributions to the Dominican economy. Their abundant, cheap labor has generated high rates of capital accumulation and vigorous competition. And second, I hope it recognizes just how much we depend on each other, that in truth there's a symbiosis between us, in construction, agriculture, tourism, in just about every industry Haitians are working in. It's time for all citizens to see the economic, social, and political reality of the island, and have the awareness they need to achieve economic self-sufficiency in a framework of mutual respect, solidarity, and fellowship."

Gabriel refilled his glass and sipped it, thinking. He left the glass on the counter and went to back to his desk. He sat down in front of his computer, and with renewed enthusiasm, pressed forward with preparing his economic thesis.

****

144

41

There were many reasons to celebrate at the Dominican chancellery, where the details of an important event were being jointly planned with Haitian authorities for September 14, 2017.

Gabriel parked his Jeep in front of the entrance to Matilde's house in Jimaní. He was attempting to unlock the door without dropping all the packages he had brought for his mom.

"But, son, why didn't you tell me you were coming?" Matilde protested when she saw him drop the assortment of boxes and bags in the living room armchair.

"So you don't start hustling and bustling, especially since I'm only going to be here for a short time."

"You just arrived, and you're already telling me you're leaving?" Matilde approached her son, and they hugged and kissed each other in greeting.

"It's that tomorrow I've got to go to Port-au-Prince to get Marcel. I want him to participate in an event I know will make him very happy. It's a surprise, so I've got to leave early to get to Port-au-Prince and come back here in time."

"So you're not going to tell me what it's about?" Matilde returned Gabriel's mischievous grin as if she were an accomplice.

"I can give you a little hint," commented Gabriel, laughing. "It has to do with something I've been trying to materialize for years."

"Umm ... materialize for years ... " Matilde sat back in the rocking chair, playing along with her son as they used to do when he was still a child. She was struck by the turns of life. Their roles were reversed; now, she felt like a child around her son.

"Well, maybe I'll give you another hint." Gabriel approached the rocking chair where Matilde sat, knelt down, and gave her a peck on the cheek. It was an effort for him to control his laughter. "I'm going to call Marcel right now."

They both laughed. Gabriel wiggled his eyebrows and began to dial Marcel's number with dramatic gestures.

"Marcel, good evening. Are you sitting down? My hands are occupied, so I'm going to use the speakerphone." Gabriel winked at Matilde.

"You sound happy! Yes, I'm sitting down. I was reading some papers. Tell me, what's up?"

"Tomorrow I'll be in Port-au-Prince, so I was wondering if we could see each other. Actually, my intention is to reciprocate what you did for me in Haiti. Can you believe that was five years ago?"

"It's amazing how time passes. I really want to see you, Gabriel. I'll make the necessary adjustments in my schedule to spend the day with you."

"Great! Just so you know, Marcel, it's something that will take three or four days. Forgive me for letting you know on such short notice, but it's something that's very important to both of us, so pack enough to spend a few days on this side of the island. We are going to celebrate."

"Then, if that's what you say, that's what we'll do," Marcel said, laughing. "I'll start making arrangements to postpone what I've got going for the next few days."

"I'll come to your house, and then we'll leave to get back here. See you tomorrow then. Get some rest."

"You too. Take care."

Gabriel smiled at his mother, who shook her head, unable to resist her son's charm.

"Yes, this is going to be a big surprise for Marcel."

"You're incorrigible," giggled Matilde.

****

When Gabriel came through Malpasse the next morning, he relived the experience of his first day in Haiti. He mentally compared the images he was now seeing to those of that overwhelming day. It all seemed like a dream. When he pulled up at Marcel's house, he began feeling quite vulnerable. Not wanting to give himself time to wonder why, he knocked on the door, and Marcel quickly answered it.

"Gabriel! Gee, boy, you haven't changed a bit! Are you sure we haven't seen each other in five years?" Marcel and Gabriel embraced and clapped one another loudly on the back.

"You look good, too. We have enough time to get out of here without killing ourselves." He paused, noticing that Marcel had lost a lot of weight.

"I love your prudence ... and your discretion," said Marcel, smiling.

Gabriel put Marcel's little suitcase in the back of the Jeep, and both climbed in. As soon as they arrived at Jimaní, Gabriel took the turn toward Santiago de los Caballeros to reach Dajabón.

"How is your health, your personal life? Whenever we've talked on the phone, we've always focused on work matters," commented Gabriel.

"I've had to change my diet completely to take care of some heart complications I developed because of my weight. I've lost about 50 pounds, and I've got 20 more to go. All the weight I put on after the earthquake in 2010."

"I know you'll do it."

"As for my personal life, well, you know how involved I am in working to bring about all the changes I want to manifest in my country's society. There are days when I have to really steel myself to go on, especially as far as the National University is concerned. Since the start of this year, the students and teachers have been on strike to demand the reopening of the eleven departments that stayed closed after the earthquake ... But then something happens, a small gesture here and there, like a sign from heaven, and my faith is renewed."

Indeed, it's like all the work being done on the National Regularization Plan for Foreigners. It's not perfect, but we've made great strides in that direction as the system becomes institutionalized. As you say, there are days when you really have to steel yourself and hang on to your faith to keep from giving up. Would you believe that out of all the migrants who sought to be regularized, we've run into the most issues with the sugarcane workers. The devil has been running loose in the sugarcane fields!"

The hours passed quickly with their entertaining, lively conversation. Then, Marcel happened to see the welcome sign to Dajabón, and he realized what Gabriel's surprise was going to be.

The new Binational Market building of Dajabón rose up in front of them. In a few minutes, Haitian and Dominican government authorities would be hosting the ribbon-cutting ceremony of this long-awaited project. Behind a long table covered with white tablecloths sat representatives of the European Delegation along with Dominican and Haitian officials, who nodded and smiled at all the guests.

"See the white-haired gentleman next to the man in the blue suit? That's Don Emilio! I'll introduce you to him. He really wants to meet you."

Marcel stared at the figure of Don Emilio Martinez Durán, the man who had meant so much to his friend. He was absorbed in his thoughts and struggling with the emotions creating a lump in his throat.

Gabriel was equally moved. He felt his heart overflowing in gratitude to God for his blessings, especially for putting him in touch with Don Emilio and Marcel, who had guided him toward the purpose of his life.

"Marcel, the seeds are germinating!" Gabriel said, his voice breaking. "This seed in particular took 30 years to sprout. But that's okay. Now, what we need to do is replicate it all along the border, and our two-headed dragon, the metaphor you love to use, will rise with force, regenerating our two countries and their relationship. With the Binational Market and the concerted action of the Dominican and Haitian governments, we will certainly gain a head, in fact two, so that mutual respect and dignity will prevail all over the island, and we will gain the wings to fly forward as brothers towards the realization and fulfillment of our aspirations in this world."

Gabriel, his tears overflowing, threw his arm around Marcel's shoulders. Deeply touched by Gabriel's words and by this poignant landmark event, he nodded and wept, convinced that in the not-too-distant future their shared dream would come true.

The End